THE ARTEMIS FOWL FILES

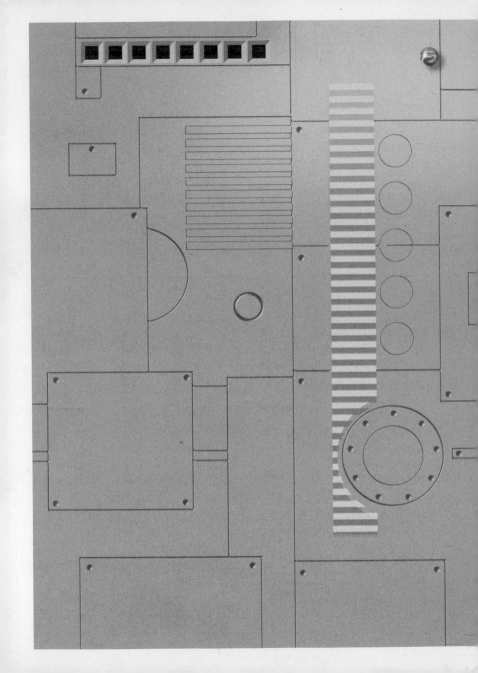

EOIN COLFER

THE ARTEMIS FOWL FILES

MIRAMAX BOOKS
HYPERION PAPERBACKS FOR CHILDREN
NEW YORK

Text copyright © 2004 by Eoin Colfer

First Hyperion Paperbacks edition, 2008

1 3 5 7 9 10 8 6 4 2

Library of Congress Cataloging-in-Publication Data on file.

ISBN-13: 978-0-7868-3675-8
ISBN-10: 0-7868-3675-X

Visit www.hyperionbooksforchildren.com

For Finn, Artemis's best friend

CONTENTS

LEPrecon

Fairy Code

Gnommish Alphabet

The People: A Spotter's Guide

Interviews

YOU

Captain Holly Short is known by everyone under the world as one of the key members of the LEPrecon Squad. But the daring young elf's job wasn't always so exciting. Like all Recon officers, she began her career in Traffic. This is the story of her initiation as a Recon captain, and how she became the first female officer to serve under Commander Julius Root.

LEPRECON

CHAPTER I: ALONG CAME A SPIDER

Sydney Harbor, Australia

"**THE** thing about pain, Major Ever-green," said the old elf, laying a small wooden case on the table, "is that it hurts."

Evergreen was still too groggy for jokes. What-ever the stranger had put in the dart was taking its time leaving his system. "What are you . . . ? Why am I . . . ?" Full sentences wouldn't come. He couldn't pluck one from his addled brain.

"Quiet, Major," advised his captor. "Don't fight the serum. You will make yourself ill."

"Serum?" gasped the major.

"A very personal concoction. Since I don't have my magic any more, I have had to rely on nature's gifts. This particular serum is concocted from equal parts ground ping-ping flower and cobra venom. Not lethal in small doses, but quite an effective sedative."

Fear was piercing the LEP officer's daze now, like a hot poker through snow. "Who are you?"

A child's scowl twisted the stranger's ancient face.

"You may address me as Captain. Don't you know me, Major? From before today? Cast your mind back to your first years in the LEP. Centuries ago, I know, but try. The fairy People often think that they can forget me completely. But I'm never far away, not really."

The major wanted to say, *Yes, I know you*, but something told him that lying would be even more dangerous than telling the truth. And the truth was that he couldn't remember seeing this old elf before in his life. Not until today, when he had assaulted him on the docks. Evergreen had tracked a runaway-gnome signal to this hut, and the next thing he knew this old elf had stung him with a syringe gun and was asking to be addressed as Captain. And now Evergreen was tied to a chair, being given a lecture about pain.

The old elf flipped two brass clasps on his case and lifted the lid reverentially. Major Evergreen caught a glimpse of a velvet lining. Red as blood.

"Now, my boy, I need information. Information only an LEP major would know." The captain lifted a leather pouch from the box. There was another box of some kind inside the bag, its edges pressing into the leather.

Evergreen's breath came in short gasps. "I'll tell you nothing."

The old elf undid the bag's leather tie with one hand. The box shone from inside the bag, casting a sickly glow on the old elf's pallor. The wrinkles around his eyes were thrown into deep shadow. The eyes themselves were feverish.

"Now, Major. The moment of truth. Question time."

"Do yourself a favor and close the bag, Captain," said Major Evergreen, with more bravado than he felt. "I am LEP: you can't harm me and hope to escape."

The captain sighed. "I cannot close the bag. What is inside yearns to come out, to be free and do its work. And don't think anyone is coming to save you. I have jacked into your helmet and sent a malfunction message. Police Plaza thinks your communications are on the blink. They won't be worried for hours."

The old elf pulled a steel object from the leather bag. The object was a mesh cage, and inside was a tiny silver spider with claws so sharp, the tips seemed to disappear. He held up the cage before Evergreen's nose. Inside, the spider slashed its claws in a starving frenzy, an inch from the major's nose.

"Sharp enough to cut air," said the captain. And indeed the claws seemed to leave short-lived rents where they passed.

The mere act of revealing the spider seemed to change the old elf. He had power now and seemed taller. Twin red dots sparked in his eyes though there was no light source in the hut. The ruffles of an old-style LEP dress uniform poked from beneath his overcoat.

"Now, my young elf, I will ask but once. Answer promptly or bear my wrath."

Major Evergreen shivered from fear and cold, but he kept his mouth tightly closed.

The captain caressed the major's chin with his cage. "Now, here is your question: where is Commander Root's next Recon initiation site?"

The major blinked sweat from his eyes. "Initiation site? Honestly, Captain, I don't know. I'm new on the squad."

The captain held the cage even closer to Evergreen's face. The silver spider lunged forward, clawing the major's cheek.

"Julius's site!" roared the captain. "Out with it!"

"No," said the major through gritted teeth. "You will not break me."

The captain's voice grew shrill with madness. "Do you see how I live? In the human world, I grow old."

Poor Major Evergreen steeled himself for death. This entire assignment had been a trap.

"Julius robbed me of Haven," raved the captain. "Evicted me like a common traitor. Exiled me to this foul cesspool of the human world. When he brings the next corporal for initiation, I will be waiting—along with a few old friends. If we cannot have Haven, then we will have our revenge."

The captain stopped his rant. He had said too much already and time was against him. He must finish this.

"You came here to search for a missing gnome: there was no gnome. We manipulated the satellite images to trap an LEP officer. I have waited two years for Julius to send a major."

It made sense. Only a major would know the locations of LEP initiations.

"And now that I have you in my clutches, you will tell me what I need to know."

The elderly elf pinched Major Evergreen's nose until he was forced to draw breath through his mouth. In a flash the captain jammed the mesh cage between Evergreen's teeth and flipped the gate. The silver spider was down the young elf's gullet in a shining blur.

The captain tossed the cage to one side. "Now, Major," he said. "You are dead."

Evergreen spasmed as the silver spider's claws went to work on the lining of his stomach.

"That feels bad: internal injuries always hurt the most," commented the old elf. "But your magic will heal you for a while. In minutes, however, your power will dry up, and then my little pet will claw her way out."

Evergreen knew it was true. The spider was a Tunnel Blue. The creature actually used its claws as teeth, pulping its meat before sucking it between its gums. Its favorite method of destruction was from the inside. A nest of these little monsters could take down a troll. One was more than enough to kill an elf.

"I can help you," said the captain. "If you agree to help me."

Evergreen gasped in pain. Whenever the spider clawed him, the magic sealed the wound, but already the healing was slowing.

"No. You'll get nothing from me."

"Fine. You die, and I will ask the next officer they send. Of course, he may refuse to cooperate too. Ah well, I have plenty of spiders."

Evergreen tried to think. He had to get out of this alive, to warn the commander. And there was only one way to do that.

"Very well. Kill the spider."

The captain grabbed Evergreen's chin. "First, my answer. Where is the next initiation? And do not lie, I will know."

"The Tern Islands," moaned the major.

The old elf's face glowed with demented triumph. "I know them. When?"

Evergreen mumbled the words, shamefacedly. "A week from today."

The captain clapped his captive on the shoulder. "Well done. You have chosen wisely. No doubt hoping to live through this ordeal and warn my brother."

Alarm cut through Evergreen's pain. Brother? This was Commander Root's brother? He had heard the story; everyone had.

The captain smiled. "Now you know my secret. I

am the disgraced Captain Turnball Root. Julius hunted his own brother. And now I shall hunt him."

Evergreen winced as a dozen tiny gashes were opened in his stomach. "Kill the insect," he pleaded.

Turnball Root drew a small flask from his pocket. "Oh, very well. But don't think you'll be warning anyone. There was an amnesiac in the dart I gave you: in five minutes this entire incident will be a dream floating beyond your grasp."

Captain Root opened the flask, and Evergreen was relieved to smell the pungent aroma of strong coffee. The Tunnel Blue was a hyperactive, finely tuned creature with a hair-trigger heart. When the coffee entered its bloodstream, it should trigger a fatal heart attack.

Turnball Root poured the scalding brew down Evergreen's throat. The major gagged, but swallowed it down. After a few seconds, the spider began to thrash in his stomach, then the vicious activity ceased.

Evergreen sighed in relief, then closed his eyes, focusing on what had happened.

"Oh, very good," chuckled Captain Root. "You are trying to reinforce the memories so they can be brought out under hypnosis. I wouldn't bother. What I gave you wasn't exactly regulation. You'll be lucky if you remember what color the sky is."

Evergreen hung his head. He had betrayed his commander, and all for nothing. In one week's time, Julius Root would walk into a trap on the Tern Islands. A location that he had revealed.

Turnball did up his overcoat, hiding the uniform below. "Farewell, Major. And thank you for your help. You may find it difficult to concentrate for the next while, but by the time your resolve returns, those straps should have dissolved."

Captain Root opened the hut door, stepping out into the night. Evergreen watched him go, and a moment later he could not have sworn that the captain had ever been there at all.

CHAPTER 2: SOMETHING FISHY

The Boulevard of Kings, Haven City,
The Lower Elements; One Week Later . . .

CORPORAL Holly Short was on traffic detail on the Boulevard of Kings. Lower Elements Police officers were supposed to travel in pairs, but there was a league crunchball match being played across the river, so her partner was patrolling the sidelines in Westside Stadium.

Holly strolled down the boulevard, resplendent in her computerized traffic suit. The suit was more or less a walking road sign that could display all the common commands, plus up to eight lines of text, across her chest plate. The suit was also coded to her voice, so if Holly ordered a driver to stop, the command would appear in yellow lights across her chest.

Being a walking road sign was not exactly what Holly had in mind when she had signed up for the Lower Elements Police Academy, but every corporal had to put in a stint in Traffic before he or she was allowed to specialize. Holly had been on the streets for over six months, and sometimes it seemed as though she was never going to get her chance at Reconnaissance. If the brass did give her a shot, and if she did pass the initiation, then she would be the first female ever to make it into Recon. This fact did not daunt Holly Short; in fact, it appealed to her stubborn nature. Not only would she pass the initiation, but she intended to smash the score set by Captain Trouble Kelp.

The boulevard was quiet this afternoon. Everyone was over in Westside enjoying vegetable fries and mushroom burgers. Everyone except her, a few dozen public servants, and the owner of a camper shuttle that was illegally parked across a restaurant's loading bay.

Holly scanned the purple camper's bar code by running her glove's sensor across the bumper plate. Seconds later, the LEP central server sent the vehicle's file to her helmet. It belonged to one E. Phyber, a sprite with a history of traffic violations.

Holly tore back a Velcro strip covering the computer screen on her wrist. She opened the parking-fine program, sending one to Phyber's account. The fact that giving someone a ticket made her feel good told Holly that it was high time she got out of Traffic.

Something moved inside the camper. Something big. The entire vehicle swayed on its axles.

Holly rapped on the blacked-out windows. "Step out of the vehicle, Mister Phyber."

There was no reply from inside the camper, just more pronounced swaying. There was something inside. Something a lot bigger than a sprite.

"Mister Phyber. Open up, or I will conduct a search."

Holly tried to peer through the tinted windows, with no luck: her street helmet did not have the filters to penetrate. It felt as though there was some kind of animal in there. This was a serious crime. Transporting animals in a private vehicle was strictly forbidden. Not to mention cruel. The fairy People might eat certain animals, but they certainly did not keep them as pets. If this person was smuggling animals of some kind, it was quite possible that he was buying them direct from the surface.

Holly placed both hands on the side panel, pushing as hard as she could. Immediately the camper began to buck and vibrate, almost tipping over on one rail.

Holly stepped back. She would have to call this in.

"Ah . . . Is there a problem, Officer?"

There was a sprite hovering beside her. Sprites hover when they are nervous.

"Is this your vehicle, sir?"

The sprite's wings beat even faster, lifting him another six inches off the sidewalk.

"Yes, Officer. Eloe Phyber. I am the registered owner."

Holly raised her visor. "Please land, sir. Flying is restricted on the boulevard. There are signs."

Phyber touched down gently. "Of course, Officer. Pardon me."

Holly studied Phyber's face for signs of guilt. The sprite's pale green skin was slick with perspiration.

"Are you worried about something, Mister Phyber?"

Phyber smiled a watery smile. "No. Worried? No, nothing. I'm running a bit late, that's all. Modern life, you know, always on a timetable."

The camper bounced on its axles.

"What have you got in there?" asked Holly.

Phyber's smile froze. "Nothing. Just some flat-packed shelving. One of the units must have fallen over."

He was lying. Holly was certain of it. "Oh really? There must be quite a few units in there, because that's the fifth one that's fallen over. Open it up, please."

The sprite's wings began pumping up. "I don't think I have to. Don't you need a warrant?"

"No. I need probable cause. And I have reason to

believe that you are illegally transporting animals."

"Animals? Ridiculous. Anyway, I can't open the camper, I appear to have lost the chip."

Holly drew an omnitool from her belt, placing the sensor against the camper's rear door. "Very well. Be advised that I am opening this vehicle to investigate the possible presence of animals."

"Shouldn't we wait for a lawyer?"

"No. The animals could die of old age."

Phyber moved back a yard. "I really wouldn't do that."

"No. I'm sure you wouldn't."

The omnitool beeped, and the rear door swung open. Holly was confronted by a huge, wobbling cube of orange jelly. It was hydrogel, used to safely transport injured sea life. The creatures could still breathe, but were spared travel bumps. A shoal of mackerel was struggling to swim inside the lined interior of the camper. They were no doubt destined for an illegal fish restaurant.

The gel might have held its shape if the shoal hadn't decided to head for the light. Their combined efforts dragged the cuboid of gel out of the camper and into thin air. Gravity took hold and the blob exploded all over Holly. She was instantly submerged in a tidal wave of fish and fish-flavored gel. The gel found holes in her uniform that she had never known were there.

"D'Arvit!" swore Holly, falling on her backside. Unfortunately this was the moment that her suit shorted out, and a call came through from Police Plaza informing her that Commander Julius Root wanted to see her immediately.

Police Plaza, the Lower Elements

Holly dropped Phyber off at the booking desk, then darted straight across the courtyard to Julius Root's office. If the LEPrecon commander wanted to see her, she had no intention of keeping him waiting. This could be her initiation. At last.

There were already people in the office. Holly could see bobbing heads through the frosted glass.

"Corporal Short to see Commander Root," she said breathlessly to the secretary.

The secretary, a middle-aged pixie with an outrageous pink perm, glanced up briefly, then stopped work completely, giving Holly her undivided attention. "You want to go in to the commander looking like that?"

Holly brushed a few blobs of hydrogel from her suit. "Yes. It's only gel. I've been on the job. The commander will understand."

"You're sure?"

"Positive. I can't miss this meeting."

The secretary's smile was tinged with nastiness. "Well, all right then. Go on in."

On any other day, Holly would have known that something was wrong, but on that day it slipped past. And so did she, right into Julius Root's office.

There were two people in the office before her. Julius Root himself, a broad-chested elf with buzz-cut hair, and a fungus cigar screwed into the corner of his mouth. Holly also recognized Captain Trouble Kelp, one of Recon's brightest stars. A legend in the police bars with more than a dozen successful recons under his belt in less than a year.

Root froze, staring at Holly. "Yes? What is it? Is there some kind of plumbing emergency?"

"N-No," stammered Holly. "Corporal Holly Short, reporting as requested, sir."

Root stood, red spots burning on his cheeks. The commander was not a happy elf.

"Short. You're a girl?"

"Yessir. Guilty as charged."

Root did not appreciate humor. "We're not on a date, Short. Keep the witticisms to yourself."

"Yessir. No jokes."

"Good. I assumed you were male because of your pilot test scores. We've never had a female score that high before."

"So I believe, sir."

The commander sat on the edge of his desk. "You are the eightieth female to have made it as far as the initiation. So far none have passed. The equal-rights office is screaming sexism, so I'm going to handle your initiation personally."

Holly swallowed. "Personally?"

Root smiled. "That's right, Corporal. Just you and me on a little adventure. How do you feel about that?"

"Great, sir. My privilege."

"Good girl. That's the spirit." Root sniffed the air. "What's that smell?"

"I was on traffic duty, sir. I had a tangle with a fish smuggler."

Root sniffed the air again. "I guessed fish were involved. Your uniform appears to be orange."

Holly picked at a blob of gel on her arm. "Hydrogel, sir. The smuggler was using it to transport the fish."

Root rose from the desk. "You do know what Recon officers actually do, Short?"

"Yessir. A Recon officer tracks runaway fairies to the surface, sir."

"The surface, Short. Where the humans live. We have to be inconspicuous, blend in. Do you think you can do that?"

"Yes, Commander. I think I can."

Root spat his cigar into a recycler. "I wish I could

believe that. And maybe I would, if it weren't for that." Root pointed a stiff finger at Holly's chest.

Holly looked down. Surely the commander wasn't upset about a few blobs of gel and the smell of fish.

He wasn't.

The text bar on her chest displayed one word in block capitals. It was the same word that she had shouted just as the hydrogel had frozen the text display: "D'Arvit," swore Holly under her breath, which coincidentally was the same word frozen on her chest.

E1

The trio proceeded directly to E1; a pressure chute that emerged in Tara, Ireland. The corporals were not given any personal time to prepare, because they would not have any if they managed to graduate to Recon. Rogue fairies did not escape to the surface at a time prearranged with the police. They took off whenever it suited them, and a Recon officer had to be ready to follow.

They took an LEP shuttle up the chute to the surface. Holly had not been given any weaponry and her helmet had been confiscated. She had also been drained of magic by a pinprick to the thumb. The tack was left in until every drop of magic had been used to heal the wound.

Captain Trouble Kelp explained the logic to her as he used his own magic to seal the corporal's tiny wound. "Sometimes you get stuck on the surface with nothing: no weapon, no communications, no magic. And you still have to track down a runner, who's probably trying to track you down. If you can't accomplish that, then you won't make it in Recon."

Holly had expected this. They had all heard the initiation stories from other veterans. She wondered what kind of hellhole they would be dropped in, and what they would have to hunt.

Through the shuttle portholes, she watched the chute flash by. The chutes were vast subterranean magma vents that spiraled from Earth's core to the surface. The fairy People had excavated several of these tunnels worldwide and built shuttle ports at both ends. As human technology grew more sophisticated, many of these stations had to be destroyed or abandoned. If the Mud People ever found a fairy port, they would have a direct line to Haven.

In times of emergency, Recon officers rode the magma flares that scoured these tunnels in titanium eggs. This was the fastest way to cover the five thousand miles to the surface. Today they were traveling as a group in an LEP shuttle at the relatively slow speed of eight hundred miles an hour. Root set the autopilot and came back to brief Holly.

"We are headed for the Tern Islands," Commander Root said, activating a holographic map above the conference table. "A small archipelago off the east coast of Ireland. To be more precise we are headed for Tern Mór, the main island. There is only one inhabitant: Kieran Ross, a conservationist. Ross travels to Dublin once a month to make his report to the Department of the Environment. He generally stays over in the Morrison Hotel, and takes in a show at the Abbey Theatre. Our technical people have confirmed that he is booked into the hotel, so we have a thirty-six-hour window."

Holly nodded. The last thing they needed was humans butting into their exercise. Realistic exercises were one thing, but not at the expense of the entire fairy nation.

Root stepped into the hologram, pointing at a spot on the map. "We land here, at Seal Bay. The shuttle will drop you and Captain Kelp off on the beach. I will be deposited at another location. After that it's simple: you hunt me and I hunt you. Captain Kelp will record your progress for review. Once the exercise has been completed, I will evaluate your disk and see if you have what it takes to make it into Recon. Initiates are generally tagged half a dozen times over the course of the exercise, so don't worry about that. What's important is how difficult you make it for me."

Root took a paintball pistol from a rack on the wall and tossed it to Holly. "Of course, there is one way to get around the review and straight into the program. You tag me before I tag you, and you're in.

No questions asked. But don't get your hopes up. I have centuries of aboveground experience, I'm running hot with magic, and I have a shuttle full of weapons at my disposal."

Holly was glad that she was already sitting down. She had spent hundreds of hours on simulators, but had only actually visited the surface twice; once on a school tour of South American rain forests, and another time on a family holiday to Stonehenge. Her third visit was going to be a bit more exciting.

CHAPTER 3: THE ISLAND OF BROKEN DREAMS

Tern Mór

THE sun scorched away the morning mist and Tern Mór gradually appeared off the Irish coast like a ghost island. One minute there was nothing there but cloud banks, and the next the crags of Tern Mór cut through the haze.

Holly studied it through the porthole. "Cheery place," she noted.

Root chewed on his cigar. "Sorry about that, Corporal. We keep asking the runaways to hide somewhere warm, but darned if they don't keep suiting themselves."

The commander returned to the cockpit: it was

time to switch back over to manual for the landing.

The island looked like something from a horror film. Dark cliffs reared from the ocean, spumes of foam slapping at the waterline. A line of greenery hung on desperately, flopping untidily over the edge like an unruly fringe of hair.

Nothing good is going to happen here, thought Holly.

Trouble Kelp slapped her on the shoulder, breaking through the gloom. "Cheer up, Short. At least you got this far. A couple of days on the surface is worth any price. This place has air like you wouldn't believe. Sweet as heaven."

Holly tried to smile, but she was too nervous. "Does the commander usually handle initiations himself?"

"All the time. This is the first one-on-one though. Usually he tracks a half dozen or so, to keep himself amused. But you get him all to yourself, 'cause of the female thing. When you fail, Julius doesn't want the equal-rights office to have any reason to complain."

Holly bristled. "When I fail?"

Trouble winked at her. "Did I say when? I meant if. Of course, if."

Holly felt the tips of her pointed ears quiver. Was this entire trip a charade? Did the commander already have her report written?

They touched down on Seal Beach, which was remarkably devoid of seals and sand. The shuttle had a second skin of plasma screens that projected the surroundings onto the craft's outer plates. To the casual observer, when Trouble Kelp popped the hatch, it would seem like a door in the sky.

Holly and Trouble hopped out onto the pebbles, scurrying forward to avoid the jet wash.

Root opened a porthole. "You've got twenty minutes to cry or say your prayers or whatever it is you females do, then I'm comin' a callin'."

Holly's eyes were fierce. "Yessir. I'm going to start crying presently. Soon as you're over the horizon."

Root half smiled, half scowled. "I hope your skills can pay the checks your mouth is writing."

Holly had no idea what a check was, but she decided that now was not the time to say that.

Root gunned the engine, taking off over the hillside in a low, looping arc. All that was visible of the craft was a faint translucent shimmer.

Holly found that she was suddenly cold. Haven was completely air-conditioned, so her traffic suit did not have heating coils. She noticed Captain Kelp adjusting the thermostat on his computer.

"Hey," Trouble said. "No need for two of us to be uncomfortable. I've already passed my initiation."

"How many times did you get tagged?" Holly asked.

Trouble grimaced ruefully. "Eight. And I was the best in the group. Commander Root moves quickly for an old-timer, plus he has a couple of million ingots worth of hardware at his disposal."

Holly turned up her collar against the Atlantic wind. "Any handy hints?"

"I'm afraid not. And once this camera starts rolling, I can't even talk to you any more." Captain Kelp touched a button on his helmet, and a red light winked at Holly. "The only thing I can say is that if I were you, I'd get moving. Julius won't waste any time, so neither should you."

Holly looked around. *Make use of your environment*, the manuals said. *Use what nature provides.* That maxim wasn't much good to her here. The pebble beach was bordered by a steep rock face on two sides, with a steep mudslide incline on the third. It was the only way out, and she'd better take it before the commander had time to set himself up at the top. She double-timed it toward the slope, determined to make it out of this exercise with her self-respect intact.

Something shimmered in the corner of Holly's eye. She stopped in her tracks.

"That's hardly fair," she said, pointing to the spot.

Trouble looked across the pebble beach. "What?" he asked, even though he was not supposed to talk.

"Look there. A sheet of cam foil. Someone is hiding on the beach. Do you have a little backup in case the corporal proves a bit quick for the old-timers?"

Trouble instantly realized the seriousness of the

situation. "D'Arvit," he growled, reaching for his sidearm.

Captain Kelp was quick on the draw. He actually managed to get his weapon out of its holster before a sniper's rifle pulsed beneath the cam foil, catching him high on the shoulder, spinning him across the wet stones.

Holly darted right, zigzagging through the rocks. If she kept moving, the sniper might not be able to get a lock on her. Her fingers were actually digging into the mud slope when a second sniper reared up from the earth, shrugging off a sheet of cam foil.

The newcomer, a stocky dwarf, was holding the biggest rifle Holly had ever seen. "Surprise," he said grinning, teeth crooked and yellowing.

He fired and the laser pulse hit Holly in the gut like a sledgehammer. That's the thing about Neutrino weapons: they don't kill, but they hurt worse than a bucket of hangnails.

Holly came to, and immediately wished she hadn't. She leaned forward on the oversize chair she was tied to, and threw up all over her boots. Beside her, Trouble Kelp was involved in the same activity. What was going on here? Laser weapons were not supposed to have side effects, unless you were allergic, which she wasn't.

Glancing around, Holly caught her breath. They were in a small roughly plastered room, dominated by a huge table. A huge table or a human-size table? They were in a human residence? That explained the sickness. Entering human residences without permission was expressly forbidden. The price for ignoring this edict was loss of magic, and nausea.

The details of their predicament sparked in Holly's memory. She had been on her initiation when a couple of fairies had ambushed them on the beach. Could this be some kind of extreme test? She looked across at Captain Kelp's drooping head. That was pretty realistic for a test.

A huge door creaked open and a grinning elf stepped through. "Oh, you are unwell. Sorcery sickness, or 'book barfing' as I believe the younger fairies call it. Don't worry, it will soon pass."

The elf looked older than any fairy Holly knew, and was wearing a yellowed LEP dress uniform. It was like something out of a period movie.

The elf caught Holly's glance. "Ah, yes," he said, plumping up his ruffles. "My finery fades. It is the curse of living without magic. Everything fades, and not just the clothing. To look in my eyes you would never guess that I am barely a century older than my brother."

Holly looked in his eyes. "Brother?"

Beside her, Trouble stirred, spat, and raised his head. Holly heard a sharp intake of breath. "Oh gods. Turnball Root."

Holly's mind spun. Root? Brother. This was the commander's brother.

Turnball was delighted. "Finally, someone remembers. I was beginning to think I was forgotten."

"I majored in Ancient History," said Trouble. "You have your own page in the 'Criminally Insane' section."

Turnball tried to appear casual, but he was interested. "Tell me, what did this page say?"

"It said that you were a traitorous captain who tried

to flood a section of Haven just to wipe out a competitor who was muscling in on your illegal mining scheme. It said that if your brother had not stopped you with your finger on the button, then half the city could have been lost."

"Ridiculous," tutted Turnball. "I had engineers study my plans. There would have been no chain reaction. A few hundred would have died, no more."

"How did you escape from prison?" asked Holly.

Turnball's chest puffed up. "I have never spent a day in prison. I am not a common criminal. Luckily, Julius lacked the gumption to kill me, and so I managed to escape. He has hunted me ever since. But that ends today."

"So that's what this is all about: revenge?"

"Partly," admitted Turnball. "But also freedom. Julius is like a dog with a bone. He will not let go. I need a chance to finish my martinis without looking over my shoulder. I have had ninety-six residences in the past five centuries. I lived in a fabulous villa near Nice in the seventeen-hundreds." The old elf's eyes grew misty. "I was so happy there. I can still smell the ocean. I had to burn that house to the ground because of Julius."

Holly was rotating her wrists slowly, trying to loosen the knots. Turnball noticed the motion.

"Don't bother, my dear. I have been tying people up for centuries. It is one of the first skills you learn as a fugitive. And well done, by the way. A female at an initiation. I bet my little brother doesn't like that. He was always a bit on the sexist side."

"Yes," said Holly. "Whereas you are a real gentle-fairy."

"Touché," said Turnball. "As I used to say in France."

Trouble's face had lost the green tinge. "What-ever your plan is, don't expect any help from me."

Turnball stood before Holly, lifting her chin with a curved nail. "I don't expect help from you, Captain. I expect help from the pretty one. All I expect from you is a little screaming before you die."

Turnball had two accomplices: a sullen dwarf and an earthbound sprite. Commander Root's brother called them into the room for a round of introductions.

The dwarf's name was Bobb, and he wore a wide-brimmed sombrero to keep the sun off his delicate dwarf skin.

"Bobb is the best burglar in the business after Mulch Diggums," explained Turnball, draping an arm round the squat dwarf's massive shoulders. "However, unlike the canny Diggums, he doesn't plan so well. Bobb made his big mistake when he dug into a community center during a police fund-raiser. He's been hiding out on the surface since then. We make a good team: I plan, he steals." He turned to the sprite, spinning him round. Where the sprite's wings should be, there were two bulbous knobs of scar tissue.

"Unix here got in a fight with a troll and lost. He was clinically dead when I found him. I gave him the last shot of magic I had to bring him back, and to this day I don't know if he loves me or hates me for it. Loyal though. This fairy here would walk into Earth's core for me."

The sprite's green features were impassive, and his eyes were as empty as wiped disks. These two fairies were the ones who had picked off Holly and Trouble on the pebble beach.

Turnball ripped Holly's name tag from her chest. "Now, here's the plan. We are going to use Corporal Short here to lure Julius in. If you try to warn him, then the captain dies in terrible agony. I have a Tunnel Blue spider in my bag that will rip his insides apart in seconds. And having entered a human dwelling, he won't have a drop of magic to ease that pain. For your part, all you have to do is sit in a clearing and wait for Julius to come and get you. When he does, then we get him. It's that simple. Unix and Bobb will accompany you. I will wait here for the happy moment when Julius is dragged through that door."

Unix cut selected straps, hauling Holly from the chair. He propelled her through the giant doorway, into the morning sunlight. Holly breathed deeply. The air was sweet here, but there wasn't a moment to pause and enjoy it.

"Why don't you run, officer?" said Unix, his voice alternately high and low, as though half broken. "Run and see what happens."

"Yeah," taunted Bobb. "See what happens."

Holly could guess what would happen. She would get another laser burst, this time in the back. She would not run. Not yet. What she would do was think and plan.

They dragged and prodded Holly across two fields that sloped southward to the cliffs. The grass was sparse and rough, like clumps of missed beard after a shave. Flocks of gulls, terns, and cormorants appeared over the cliff line like fighter jets climbing to cruising altitude. Down past a thicket rampant with wildlife, Bobb stopped beside a low rock erupting through the earth. Just big enough to shelter one fairy from an easterly approach.

"Down you go,' he grunted, pushing Holly onto her knees.

Once she was down, Unix clamped a manacle round her leg, hammering the spike on the other end into the earth.

"This way, you can't just take off," he explained, grinning. "If we see you playing with your chain, then we knock you out for a while." He patted the scope on the rifle strapped across his chest. "We'll be watching."

The rogue fairies retraced their steps across the field, settling down into two hollows. They pulled sheets of cam foil from their packs, draping them over their frames. In seconds all that could be seen were two black-eyed gun barrels poking from beneath the sheets.

It was a simple plan. But extremely clever. If the commander found Holly, it would seem as though she were setting herself up for an ambush. Just not a very good one. The second he showed himself, Unix and Bobb could nail him with rifle fire.

There must be some way to warn the commander without endangering Trouble. Holly chewed it over. *Use what nature provides*. Nature was providing plenty, but unfortunately she couldn't reach any of it. If she even tried, then Bobb and Unix would stun her with a low-level charge, without having to alter the basic structure of their plan. There was nothing much on her own person either. Unix had searched her from head to toe, even confiscating the digi-pen so she couldn't try to use it as a weapon. The only thing they missed was the wafer-thin computer on her wrist, which was shorted out anyway.

Holly lowered her arm behind the rock, peeling back the Velcro patch that protected her computer from the elements. She flipped the tiny instrument over. It seemed as though hydrogel had seeped into the seal, shorting out the electrics. She slid off the battery panel, checking the circuit board inside. A tiny drop of gel was sitting on the board, straddling several switches, making connections where there shouldn't be any. Holly plucked a blade of coarse grass, using it to scoop up the drop. In less than a minute the remaining film of gel had evaporated and the tiny computer hummed into action. Holly quickly blacked out the panel on her chest, so Bobb and Unix wouldn't spot the flashing cursor.

So, now she had a computer. If she only had her helmet, she could send the commander an e-mail. As it was, all she could do was run some text across her chest.

CHAPTER 4: BROTHERS WITH ARMS

Tern Mór, Northern Peninsula

 Julius Root was surprised to find that he was breathing hard. There was a time when he could have run all day without breaking a sweat, and now his heart was battering his ribcage after a mere two-mile jog. He had parked the shuttle on a foggy cliff top on the island's northern peak. Of course, the fog was artificial, generated by a compressor bolted onto the shuttle's exhaust. The shuttle's projection shield was still in operation, the fog was merely a backup.

Root ran low, bent almost double. A hunter's run. As he moved he felt the primal joy that only surface air could bring. The sea crashed on all sides; an everpresent behemoth, a reminder of Earth's power. Commander Julius Root was never happier than when he was on the hunt aboveground. Strictly speaking, he could have delegated these initiations, but he wouldn't give up these excursions until the first rookie beat him. It hadn't happened yet.

Nearly two hours later the commander paused, taking a deep swallow from a canteen. This hunt would have been much easier with a pair of mechanical wings, but in the name of fair play he had left the wings on their rack in the shuttle. He would not have anyone claim that he had beaten them with superior equipment.

Root had searched all the obvious sites, and had yet to find Corporal Short. Holly had not been on the beach, or in the old quarry. Neither had she been perched in a treetop in the evergreen wood. Perhaps she was smarter than the average cadet. She would need to be. For a female to survive in Recon, she would have to rise above a lot of suspicion and prejudice. Not that the commander was tempted to cut her any slack. He would treat her with the same brash disdain that all his subordinates got. Until they earned something better.

Root continued his search, senses alert to any change in his surroundings that could indicate he himself was being tracked. The two hundred or so species of birds that nested on Tern Mór's crags were unusually active. Gulls screeched at him from overhead, crows followed his movements, and Julius even spotted an eagle spying at him from the heavens. All this noise made it more difficult for him to concentrate, but the distraction would be even worse for Corporal Short.

Root jogged up a shallow incline toward the human dwelling. Short could not be inside the actual dwelling itself, but she could be using it for cover. The commander hugged the thicket, his dull green LEP jumpsuit blending with the foliage.

Julius heard something up ahead. An irregular scraping. The noise of fabric against rock. He froze, then slowly twisted his way into the foliage itself. A disgruntled rabbit turned tail, wriggling deeper into the hedgerow. Root ignored the brambles dragging at his elbows, inching forward toward the source of the noise. It could be nothing, but on the other hand it could be everything.

It turned out to be everything. From his shelter inside the thicket, Root could clearly see Holly hunkered behind a large rock. It wasn't a particularly clever hiding place. She was sheltered from an easterly approach, but otherwise she was wide open. Captain Kelp was not visible, possibly filming from a raised vantage point.

Root sighed. He was surprised to find that he was disappointed. It would have been nice to have a girl around the place. Someone new to shout at.

Julius drew his paintball pistol, poking the barrel through spirals of briar branches. He would tag her a couple of times just to make an impression. Short had better wake up and do better if she ever wanted the Recon insignia on her lapel.

There was no need for Root to use the sights on his helmet. It was an easy shot, barely twenty feet. And even if it hadn't been, Root would not have used his visor. Short didn't have electronic sights, so he wouldn't use them either. This would give him even more to shout about after the failed initiation.

Then Holly turned in the direction of the thicket. She still couldn't see him, but he could see her. And even more important, he could read the words scrolling across her chest.

TURNBALL + 2

Commander Root drew his gun barrel back into the thicket, retreating into the blackness of the overgrowth.

Root battled to contain his emotions. Turnball was back. And he was here. How was it possible? All the old feelings quickly resurfaced, lodging in the commander's stomach. Turnball was his brother, and a nub of affection for him still remained. But the overriding emotion was sadness. Turnball had betrayed the People, and had been willing to see many of them die for his own profit. He had allowed his brother to escape once before; he would not let it happen again.

Root wiggled backward through the thicket, then activated his helmet. He tried establishing a link with Police Plaza, but all he got on the helmet radio was white noise. Turnball must have detonated a jammer.

Turnball may control the airwaves, but he could not control the air itself. And any living thing would heat the air. Root lowered a thermal filter on his visor and began a slow grid search of the area behind Corporal Short.

The commander's search did not take too long. Two red slits shone like beacons among the pale pink of insect and rodent life teeming under the field's surface. The slits were probably caused by a body-heat leakage from underneath two sheets of cam foil. Snipers. Lying in wait for him. These fairies were not professional. If they had been, they would have kept their gun barrels beneath the sheet until they were needed, thus eliminating the heat spill.

Root holstered his paintball pistol, drawing instead a Neutrino 500. Usually in combat situations he carried a tri-barreled water-cooled blaster, but he hadn't been expecting combat. He berated himself silently. Idiot. Combat does not arrange itself around schedules.

The commander circled round behind the snipers, then put two bursts into them from a distance. This might not have been the most sporting course of action, but it was definitely the most prudent. By the time the snipers regained consciousness they would be shackled to each other in the back of a police shuttle. If by some chance he had stunned two innocents, then there would be no lasting aftereffects.

Commander Root trotted to the first hide, drawing back the sheet of cam foil. There was a dwarf in the hollow beneath. An ugly little spud. Root recognized him from his Wanted sheet. Bobb Ragby. A nasty character. Just the kind of dim-witted felon Turnball would recruit to his cause. Root knelt by the dwarf, disarming him and zipping plasti-cuffs round his wrists and ankles.

He quickly crossed the fifty yards to the second sniper. Another well-known fugitive: Unix B'Lob. The grounded sprite. He had been Turnball's right-hand fairy for decades now. Root grinned tightly as he bound the unconscious sprite. Even just these two would be a good day's work. But the day wasn't over yet.

Holly was surreptitiously worming the spike from the ground when Root arrived.

"Can I give you a hand with that?" asked Julius.

"Get down, Commander," hissed Holly. "There are two rifles trained on you right now."

Root patted the guns slung over his shoulder. "You mean these rifles. I got your text. Well done." He wrapped his fingers round the chain, yanking it from the earth. "The parameters of your assignment have changed."

You don't say, thought Holly.

Root used an omnitool to pop open the shackle. "This is no longer an exercise. We are now in a combat situation, with a hostile and presumably armed opponent."

Holly rubbed her ankle where the shackle had chafed. "Your brother, Turnball, has Captain Kelp in the human dwelling. He has threatened to feed him a

Tunnel Blue spider if anything goes wrong with the plan."

Root sighed, leaning against the rock. "We can't go inside the dwelling. If we do, not only will we get disorientated, but the arrest won't be legal. Turnball is clever. Even if we did outsmart his goons, we couldn't take the house."

"We could use laser sights and knock out the target," suggested Holly. "Then Captain Kelp could walk out himself."

If the target had been anyone else besides his own brother, Root would have smiled. "Yes, Corporal Short. We could do that."

Root and Holly double-timed it to a ridge overlooking the human dwelling. The cottage was in a hollow, surrounded by silver birch trees.

The commander scratched his chin. "We have to get closer. I need to get a clean shot through one of the windows. One chance may be all we get."

"Should I take one rifle, sir?" asked Holly.

"No. You're not licensed for weapons. Captain

Kelp's life is at stake here, so I need steady fingers on the trigger. And even if you did bag Turnball, it would blow our entire case."

"So what can I do?"

Root checked the load in both weapons. "Stay here. If Turnball gets me, then go back to the shuttle and activate the distress signal. If help doesn't arrive and you see Turnball coming, then set the self-destruct."

"But I can fly the shuttle," protested Holly. "I have hundreds of hours on the simulators."

"And no pilot's licence," added the commander. "If you fly that thing, you may as well kiss your career good-bye. Set the self-destruct, then wait for the Retrieval squad." He handed Holly the starter chip, which doubled as a locator. "That's a direct order, Short, so take that insolent look off your face, it's making me nervous. And when I get nervous I tend to fire people. Get the message?"

"Yessir. Message understood, sir."

"Good."

Holly squatted behind the ridge while her commander threaded his way through the trees toward the house itself. Halfway down the hill, he buzzed up his shield, becoming all but invisible to the naked eye. When a fairy shielded, he vibrated so quickly that the eyes could not capture an image of him. Of course, Root would have to turn off his shield to take the shot at his brother, but that need not be until the last moment.

Root could taste metal filings in the air, doubtless left over from the radio jammer that Turnball had detonated earlier. He stepped carefully over the uneven terrain until the front windows of the house were clearly visible. The curtains were open, but there was no sign of Turnball or Captain Kelp. Round the back then.

Hugging the wall, the commander crept along the cracked flagstone path to the rear of the cottage. Trees lined both sides of a narrow unkempt yard. And there, perched on a stool on the flagstone patio, was his brother, Turnball, face lifted to the morning sun without a care in the world.

Root's breath caught and his step faltered. His only brother. Flesh of his flesh. For a moment, the commander imagined what it would be like to embrace his brother and wash away the past, but the moment quickly passed. It was too late for reconciliation. Fairies had almost died, and still could.

Root raised his weapon, training the barrel on his brother. It was a ridiculously easy shot for even a mediocre marksman. He could not believe that his brother had been stupid enough to expose himself in this way. As he crept closer, Julius was saddened by how old Turnball looked. There was barely a century between them, and yet his older brother looked as though he had barely enough energy to stand. Longevity was part of fairy magic, and without magic, time had taken a premature hold on Turnball.

"Hello, Julius, I can hear you there," said Turnball, without opening his eyes. "The sun is glorious, is she not? How can you live without her? Why don't you unshield? I haven't seen your face for so long."

Root relaxed his shield and fought to keep his aim steady. "Shut up, Turnball. Just don't speak to me. You're a convict-to-be, that's all. Nothing more."

Turnball opened his eyes. "Ah, little brother. You

don't look well. High blood pressure. No doubt brought on by hunting for me."

Julius couldn't help being drawn into conversation. "Look who's talking. You look like a rug that's been beaten once too often. And still wearing the old LEP uniform, I see. We don't have ruffled collars any more, Turnball. If you were still a captain, you'd know that."

Turnball fluffed his collar. "Is that really what you want to talk to me about, Julius? Uniforms? After all this time."

"We'll have plenty of time to talk when I visit you in prison."

Turnball extended his wrists dramatically. "Very well, Commander. Take me away."

Julius was suspicious. "Just like that? What are you up to?"

"I'm tired," sighed his brother. 'I"m tired of life among the Mud People. They are such barbarians. I want to go home, even if it is to a cell. You have obviously dispatched my helpers, so what choice do I have?"

Root's soldier's intuition was pounding like a bell clapper inside his skull. He dropped the thermal filter in his visor and saw that there was only one other fairy in the dwelling. Someone tied in a sitting position. That must be Captain Kelp.

"And where is the delightful Corporal Short?" asked Turnball casually.

Root decided to leave himself an ace in the hole, in case he needed it. "Dead," he spat. "Your dwarf shot her when she warned me. That's another charge you will have to answer for."

"What's another charge? I only have one life to spend in captivity. You'd better hurry up and arrest me, Julius. Because if you don't, I may go back inside the house."

Julius had to think quickly. It was obvious that Turnball had something planned. And he would probably make his move when Julius zipped on the cuffs. Then again he couldn't make a move if he was unconscious.

Without a word of warning, the commander hit his brother with a low-level charge. Just enough to knock him out for a few moments. Turnball slumped backward, a surprised look on his face.

Root holstered his Neutrino and hurried toward his brother. He wanted Turnball trussed like a solstice turkey when he came to. Julius took three steps, then he didn't feel so well. A pounding headache landed on him like a lead weight from a height. Sweat popped from every pore and his sinuses were instantly blocked. What was going on here? Root dropped to his knees, then all fours. He felt like throwing up, then sleeping for eight hours. His bones had turned to jelly and his head weighed a ton. Every breath sounded amplified and distant.

The commander stayed in that position for over a minute, completely helpless. A kitten could have knocked him over and stolen his wallet. He could only watch as Turnball regained consciousness, shook his head to dislodge the afterbuzz, then began to smile slowly.

Turnball rose, towering above his helpless brother. "Who is the smart one?" he shouted at his stricken brother. "Who has always been the smart one?"

Root could not answer. All he could do was try to marshal his thoughts. It was too late for his body: that had betrayed him.

"Jealousy," proclaimed Turnball, spreading his arms. "This has always been about jealousy. I am better than you in every way, and you can't handle it." The madness was in his eyes now, and flecks of spittle spattered onto his chin and cheeks.

Root managed two words: "You're insane."

"No," said Turnball. "What I am is fed up. I am fed up with running away from my own brother. The whole thing is too melodramatic. So, much as it pains me to do it, I am going to take your edge away from you. I am going to take your magic. Then you will be like me. I've already started, would you like to know how?"

Turnball took a tiny remote control from the pocket of his great coat. He pressed a button, and glass walls shimmered into view all round the brothers. They were no longer outside in the garden, they were inside a conservatory. Root had entered through open double doors.

"Naughty, Commander," admonished Turnball. "You entered a human dwelling without an invitation. That is against the rules of our religion. You do that a few more times, and your magic will be gone forever."

Root's head hung lower. He had waltzed into Turnball's trap, like a raw recruit two days out of the Academy. His brother had rigged a few sheets of cam foil and some projectors to disguise the conservatory, and he had fallen for it. His only hope now was Holly Short. And if Turnball had outwitted Captain Kelp and himself, what chance did a girl have?

Turnball grabbed Root by the scruff of the neck, dragging him toward the house. "You don't look so well," he said, his voice loaded with false concern. "We'd better get you inside."

CHAPTER 5: CAREER OR COMRADES?

 HOLLY watched the commander's capture from the ridge. When Root went down, she jumped to her feet and sprinted down the hillside, fully prepared to disobey her orders and go to the commander's aid. Then the conservatory shimmered into view, stopping Holly in her tracks. She would be of no use inside the house boundaries, unless she could somehow save the commander by vomiting. There had to be another way.

Holly turned, crawling back uphill on all fours, digging her fingers into the earth, dragging herself toward the wood. Once under cover, she activated the locator in the shuttle's starter chip. Her orders were to return to the craft and send a distress signal.

Eventually it would penetrate the jammer's waffle. Though by then, it would probably be too late.

She ran across the wild fields, rough grass grabbing at her boots. Birds circled overhead, their desperate cackling somehow echoing her own mood. The wind pushed in her face, slowing her pace. Even nature seemed to be against the LEP on this day.

The locator beep led her across a thigh-high stream. The freezing waters slashed through gaps in Holly's suit, pouring over her legs. She ignored it, and a trout the size of her arm who seemed very interested in the material of her suit. She battled on, over a human-size stile and up a steep hill. Low-lying fog sat on the hilltop like whipped cream on a wedge of cake.

Holly could smell the fog before she reached it. It was chemical. Manufactured. The shuttle was obviously inside the cloud bank.

With the last vestiges of her strength, Holly batted aside sheets of clinging fake fog and remote-activated the shuttle door. She collapsed inside, lying prone on the bay doors for a brief moment, drawing in huge breaths. Then she clambered to her feet and slapped the emergency button on the dash, activating the emergency beam.

The beam icon winked on, followed by a huge anticlimax. All Holly could do was sit there watching failure messages flash onto the plasma screen. Here she was, sitting on millions of ingots' worth of technology, and her orders were to do nothing.

Captain Kelp and Commander Root were in mortal danger, and her orders were to twiddle her thumbs. If she flew the shuttle she would be in breach of a direct order, and her career in Recon would be over before it began. But if she didn't fly it, then her comrades were dead. Which was more important, career or comrades?

Holly stuffed the starter chip into the ignition slot and strapped herself in.

Turnball Root was enjoying himself immensely. Finally the moment he had dreamed about for so many decades had arrived. His baby brother was at his mercy.

"I thought I might keep you here for the next

twenty-four hours until your magic is completely gone. Then we will become true brothers again. A real team. Perhaps you will decide to join me. If not, you certainly won't be leading the chase. The LEP do not employ personnel without magic."

Root was curled up in a ball on the floor, his face greener than a sprite's behind. "Dream on," he grunted. "You're no brother of mine."

Turnball pinched his cheek. "You'll warm to me, little brother. It's amazing who a fairy turns to in times of desperation. Believe me, I know."

"In your dreams."

Turnball sighed. "Still obstinate. You are probably entertaining notions of escape. Or perhaps you believe that in the end, I could never hurt my baby brother. Is that it? You believe that I have a heart? Perhaps a small demonstration . . ."

Turnball lifted Captain Kelp's head from his chest. Trouble was barely conscious. He had been in the house for too long. He would never run at a hundred percent of his magical potential again. Not without an infusion from a team of warlocks. And soon.

Turnball held a small cage up to Trouble's face. Inside, a Tunnel Blue spider scratched at the mesh.

"I like these creatures," said Turnball gently. "They will go through anything to survive. They remind me of myself. This little one will make short work of the captain here."

Root tried to raise a hand. "Turnball, don't."

"I must," said Turnball. "Think of it as already done. There is nothing you can do."

"Turnball. It's murder."

"Murder is a word. Just another word."

Turnball Root began wiggling the tiny bolt. Barely an inch of metal was left to hold the hatch, when a spearlike communications spike punctured the roof, embedding itself in the floorboards. Holly's amplified voice boomed from the speaker in the shaft, shaking the entire house.

"Turnball Root," said the voice. "Release your prisoners and surrender."

Turnball reset the bolt, pocketing the cage. "The girl is dead, eh? When are you going to stop lying to me, Julius?"

Julius was too weak to respond. The world had become a bad dream. He was breathing treacle.

Turnball turned his attention to the com spike. He knew that the instrument would broadcast his words to the shuttle above.

"The pretty corporal, alive and well. Ah well, no matter. You cannot come in, and I will not go out. If you do enter, I will go free. Not only that, but I will have gained a shuttle. If you try to detain me when I am ready to leave, then my arrest will be illegal and my lawyer will carve you up like a whale in a human boat."

"I will blast that house to kingdom come," warned Holly, through the com spike.

Turnball spread his arms. "Blast away. You will put me out of my misery. But when the first bolt hits, I will feed my spider to the commander. The Root brothers will not be surviving this assault. Face it, Corporal. You cannot win as long as this house stands."

Overhead in the shuttle, Holly realized that Turnball had all the angles covered. He knew the LEP rulebook better than she did. Even though she was the one with the aircraft, Turnball was the one with the upper hand. If she broke the rules, then he simply walked away and took off in his own shuttle, which was no doubt concealed somewhere close by.

"You cannot win as long as this house stands."

He was right. She couldn't win as long as a human dwelling surrounded her fellow LEP officers. But what if there were no dwelling?

Holly quickly checked the shuttle's specs. It had the standard docking clamps prow and aft. The clamps allowed the shuttle to be reeled in for landing on uneven terrain, but could also be used to tow vehicles, or possibly for other more unconventional operations.

"You cannot win as long as this house stands."

Holly felt sweat break out on the nape of her neck. Was she crazy? Could what she had planned ever stand up in court? It didn't matter, she decided. Lives were at stake.

She flipped the safety covers from the prow clamps, angling the shuttle so that the nose was pointing at the fisherman's cottage.

"Final warning, Turnball," Holly said into the

com spike. "Are you coming out?"

"Not just yet, my dear," came the cheerful reply. "But do feel free to come in and join us."

Holly did not bother with more conversation. She deployed the prow clamps with the flick of a switch. The clamps on this particular model were operated by opposing magnetic fields, and there was a slight pulse in the readouts as the two cylindrical clamps rocketed from the belly of the shuttle and straight through the roof of the cottage.

Holly set the cable for twenty yards so the clamps would not reach head height. Gripper claws extended from the clamps, grasping wooden joists, floorboards, and plaster. Holly retracted the clamps, discarding the detritus. Most of the roof was gone, and the south wall teetered dangerously. Holly took a quick photo and ran it through the computer for analysis.

"Computer," she said. "Verbal query."

"Proceed," said the computer in the tones of Foaly, the LEP's technical wizard.

"Locate load-bearing points."

"Locating."

In seconds the computer had reduced the photograph to a 3D line representation. Four red dots pulsed gently on the drawing. If she could hit any one, the entire house would collapse. Holly looked closer. Demolition had been one of her favorite classes at the Academy, and she could see that if she took out the first-floor crossbeam on the gable end, then what was left of the house would collapse outward.

Turnball was ranting into the com spike. "What are you playing at?" he roared. "You can't do this. It's against regulations. Even if you tear off the roof, you can't come into this house."

"What house?" said Holly, and fired the third clamp.

The clamp grabbed the beam and ripped it right out of the brickwork. The house groaned like a mortally wounded giant, then shuddered and collapsed. The collapse was almost comical in its suddenness, and barely a brick fell inward. Turnball Root was left with nowhere to hide.

Holly put a laser dot on Turnball's chest. "Take one step," she said, "and I will blast you into the ocean."

"You can't shoot me," Turnball retorted. "You're not certified for combat."

"No," said a voice beside him. "But I am."

Trouble Kelp was on his feet, dragging the enormous chair behind him. He launched himself at Turnball Root, and they went down in a tangle of wooden and flesh-and-bone legs.

Overhead in the shuttle, Holly slapped the dash. She had been quite prepared to knock out Turnball Root with a laser sting; after all, it was a little late to start worrying about regulations. She piloted the shuttle to a safe distance, and swooped in for landing.

In the cottage ruins, Commander Root's strength was slowly returning. Now that the human dwelling was effectively destroyed, the magic sickness was receding fast. He coughed, shook his head, and climbed to his knees.

Trouble was fighting with Turnball in the rubble. Fighting and losing. Turnball might be older, but he was possessed and lucid. He smashed blow after blow into the captain's face.

Julius picked up a rifle from the floor. "Give it

up, Turnball," he said tiredly. "It's over."

Turnball's shoulders sagged, and he turned slowly. "Ah, Julius. Little brother. It's come to this, once more. Brother against brother."

"Stop talking, please. Lie flat on the ground with your hands behind your head. You know the position."

Turnball did not lie down, instead he stood slowly, talking seductively all the time. "This doesn't have to be the end. Just let me go. I'll be out of your life forever. You'll never hear from me again, I swear it. This whole thing was a mistake, I see that now. I regret it, sincerely."

Root's energy was returning, bolstering his resolve. "Shut up, Turnball, or so help me I will blast you where you stand."

Turnball smiled easily. "You can't kill me: we're family."

"I don't have to kill you, just knock you out. Now look into my eyes and tell me I wouldn't do that."

Turnball searched his brother's eyes and found the truth there.

"I can't go to prison, brother. I'm not a common criminal. Prison would make me run of the mill."

In a flash, Turnball reached into his pocket for the tiny mesh cage. He released the bolt and swallowed the spider. "There was an old man who swallowed a spider," he said, and then; "Good-bye, brother."

Root crossed the ruined kitchen in three paces. He ripped open a fallen cupboard, searching among the foodstuffs. He grabbed a jar of instant coffee and spun the lid off. In two more paces he was kneeling beside his fallen brother, forcing handfuls of coffee grains down his throat.

"It's not going to be that easy, Turnball. You are a common criminal, and you will go to jail like one."

After a moment Turnball stopped jerking. The spider was dead. The old elf was hurt, but alive. Root quickly zipped him up in a pair of cuffs, then hurried to Trouble's side.

The captain was already sitting up. "No offence, Commander, but your brother hits like a pixie."

Root nearly smiled. "Lucky for you, Captain."

Holly rushed down the garden path, through

what had once been a parlor, and into the kitchen.

"Is everything all right?"

Root had had an unusually stressful day, and unfortunately Holly caught some of the overspill.

"No, Short, everything is not all right," he barked, brushing dust from his lapels. "My exercise has been hijacked by a notorious criminal, my captain has allowed himself to be tied up like a prize pig, and you have disobeyed a direct order and flown a shuttle. This means that our entire case is blown."

"Just this case," said Trouble. "He still has several lifetimes to serve for past crimes."

"That is beside the point," continued Root, unrelenting. "I cannot trust you, Short. You saved us, it's true, but Recon is all about stealth, and you are not a stealthy fairy. It might seem unreasonable after all you've done, but I'm afraid there is no place for you in my squad."

"Commander," objected Trouble. "You can't flunk the girl after all this. If it wasn't for her I'd be bio-degrading right now."

"This is not your decision, Captain. Nor is it

your fight. This squadron is all about trust, and Corporal Short did not earn mine."

Trouble was flabbergasted. "Pardon me, sir, but you haven't given her a fair chance."

Root glanced sharply at his officer. Trouble was one of his best fairies, and he was putting his neck on the block for this girl.

"Very well, Short. If you can do anything to change my mind, now is your chance. Your only chance. Well, can you do anything?"

Holly looked at Trouble, and she could have sworn that he winked at her. This gave her the courage to do something unthinkable, ridiculously impertinent, and insubordinate given the circumstances.

"Just this, Commander," she said.

Holly drew her paintball pistol and shot Commander Julius Root three times in the chest. The impact knocked him back a step.

"'You tag me before I tag you, and you're in,'" mumbled Holly. "No questions asked."

Trouble laughed until he threw up. Literally. The magic sickness had left him nauseous. "Oh gods," he panted. "She got you there, Julius. That's what you said. That's what you've been saying for the past hundred years."

Root ran a finger through the congealing paint on his chest plate.

Holly stared at her toes, convinced that she was about to be slung out of the force altogether. To the left, Turnball was calling for his lawyer. Flocks of protected birds were whirling overhead, and out in the fields Unix and Bobb would be wondering what had hit them.

Holly finally risked an upward glance. The commander's features were twisted with conflicting emotions. Anger was in there, and disbelief too. And maybe, just maybe, a touch of admiration.

"You did tag me," he said finally.

"That's right," agreed Trouble. "She did."

"And I did say . . ."

"You certainly did."

Root rounded on Trouble. "What are you? A parrot? Will you shut your trap? I'm trying to swallow my pride here."

Trouble locked his lips, throwing away the imaginary key.

"This is going to cost the department a fortune, Short. We're going to have to rebuild here, or generate a localized tidal wave to cover the damage. That's six months of my budget right there."

"I know, sir," said Holly humbly. "Sorry, sir."

Root drew out his wallet, taking a set of silver acorns from a compartment. He tossed them to Holly, who almost missed the catch in her surprise.

"Put them on. Welcome to Recon."

"Thank you, sir," said Holly, clipping the insignia to her lapel. It caught the rising sun and flashed like a satellite.

"The first female in Recon," groaned the commander.

Holly lowered her face to hide a grin that she couldn't contain.

"You're going to wash out in six months," continued Root, "and probably cost me a fortune."

He was wrong about the first, but right about the second.

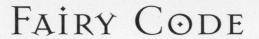

FAIRY CODE

The fairy Book, written in Gnommish, contains the history and the secrets of the People. Until now, Artemis Fowl was the only human who could read the ancient language. With the key on page 77, now you too can reveal the following ancient piece of advice:

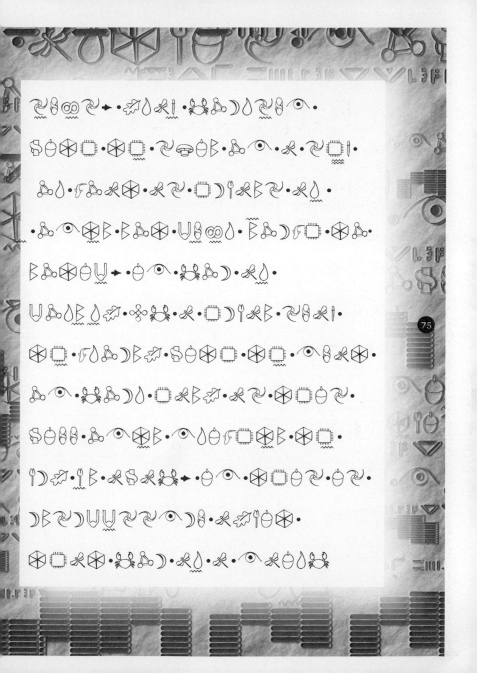

THE PEOPLE:
A SPOTTER'S GUIDE

ELVES

Distinguishing features:
About three feet tall
Pointy ears
Brown skin
Red hair

Character:
Intelligent
Strong sense of right and wrong
Very loyal
Sarcastic sense of humor, although that might just be
    characteristic of one particular female LEP officer

Loves:
Flying, either in a craft or with wings

Situations to avoid:
They really don't like it if you kidnap them and take
their gold.

There are many different types of fairy and, with each one, it's important to know what you are dealing with. This is just some of the information collected by Artemis Fowl during his adventures. It is confidential and must *not* fall into the wrong hands. The future of the People depends on it.

DWARFS

Distinguishing features:
Short, round, and hairy
Large tombstone teeth—good for grinding . . . well, anything really
Unhingable jaws enabling them to excavate tunnels
Sensitive beard hair
Skin capable of acting like suction cups when dehydrated
Smelly

Character:
Sensitive
Intelligent
Criminal tendencies

Loves:
Gold and precious gems
Tunneling
The dark

Situations to avoid:
Being in a confined space with them when they have been tunneling and have a buildup of trapped air. If they reach for the bum flap on their trousers, get out of there. . . .

†ROLLS

Distinguishing features:
Huge—as big as an elephant
Light-sensitive eyes
Hate noise
Hairy, with dreadlocks
Retractable claws
Teeth!—lots and lots of teeth
Tusks like a wild boar (a really wild boar)
Green tongue
Exceptionally strong
Weak point at the base of the skull

Character:
Very, very stupid—trolls have tiny brains
Mean and bad-tempered

Loves:
Eating—anything. A couple of cows would make
a light snack

Situations to avoid:
Are you joking? If you even think a troll is near, run like the
wind.

Goblins

Distinguishing features:
Scaly
Lidless eyes—they lick their eyeballs to keep them moist
Able to throw fireballs
They go on all fours when speed is important
Forked tongue
Less than three feet tall
Slimy, fireproof skin

Character:
Not clever, but cunning
Argumentative
Ambitious
Power-hungry

Loves:
Fire
A good argument
Power

Situations to avoid:
Don't get in the way if they're throwing a fireball.

Centaurs

Distinguishing features:
Half man, half pony
Hairy—obviously!
Hooves can get very dry

Character:
Extremely intelligent
Vain
Paranoid
Kind
Computer geek

Loves:
Showing off
Inventing

Situations to avoid:
They aren't very dangerous physically, but they will sulk if you criticize their latest invention, mess with their hard drive, or borrow their hoof moisturizer.

Sprites

Distinguishing features:
About three feet tall
Pointy ears
Green skin
Wings

Character:
Average intelligence
Generally happy-go-lucky attitude

Loves:
Flying—more than anything else under or above the earth

Situations to avoid:
Watch out for low-flying sprites—they don't always look where they're going.

Pixies

Distinguishing features:
About three feet tall
Pointy ears
Apart from their ears and their height, pixies look
   almost human

Character:
Extremely intelligent
No morals
Cunning
Ambitious
Greedy

Loves:
Power and money
Chocolate

Situations to avoid:
Never get on the wrong side of a pixie, especially one as clever and ruthless as Opal Koboi, unless you are as brilliant as Artemis Fowl, of course.

INTERVIEW WITH
ARTEMIS FOWL II

If you weren't a criminal mastermind, what would you most like to do?

I think there is a lot of work to be done in the field of psychology. If I did not have my criminal plots to occupy my time, I think I would devote my energies to putting right some of the mistakes made by misters Freud and Jung.

What do you really think of Captain Holly Short?

I have immense respect for Captain Short and I often wish she would come over to my side, as it were. But I know she never will. She has too many principles. And if she ever lost those principles, perhaps I would lose my respect for her, too.

You have traveled a great deal. Where is your favorite place in the world, and why?

My favorite place in the world is Ireland. As the fairy People say, it is the most magical place. Its landscapes are the most inspirational in the world. And the people are witty and genuine, though we do have a dark side.

What was your most embarrassing moment?

I once scored a mere ninety-nine percent on a mathematics assignment. I was mortified. I had forgotten to round up the third decimal place. Imagine my embarrassment.

What is your favorite book?

My favorite book this week is *The Lord of the Flies* by William Golding. It is a fascinating psychological study of a group of boys stranded on an island. I can't help thinking that if I had been on that island, I would be running the place in a week.

What is your favorite song?

I rarely listen to popular music, with the exception of David Bowie, who is quite a chameleon. One never knows quite what to expect. I think Bowie is a fascinating individual and I am thinking of approaching him with a scheme of mine for rediscovering a lost Mozart opera, which, of course, I have written. My favorite song of Mister Bowie's is "It's No Game, Part 2," from the *Scary Monsters* CD.

What keeps you awake at night?

My plans. They run around my head at night, keeping me awake. There is one more thing that keeps me awake. Sometimes I feel bad about the things I have done. If this feeling of guilt strikes, I do a quick online check of my bank balance, and it soon goes away.

What is your most treasured possession?

My most treasured possession is a cache of LEP equipment that Butler confiscated from a fairy Retrieval team. There are a thousand inventions in there that have never been seen by humans. These will be my retirement fund.

Who is your best friend?

I believe that we agreed that this question would not be asked. If my enemies discovered who my best friend is, they could get to me through him or her. Let me just say that my best friend is never far away and has been with me since the day of my birth.

INTERVIEW WITH
CAPTAIN
HOLLY SHORT

Do you mind being the only female elf in the LEPrecon Unit?

Some days it's a pain. It would be nice to have a female colleague to talk to at the end of a long shift. In the beginning some of the male officers used to give me a hard time. Now they're too busy chasing my flight records to insult me.

What was your proudest moment?

My proudest moment was when we shut down the goblin revolution. If those scaly gangsters had managed to take over Police Plaza, our entire culture would have been destroyed.

What was your most embarrassing moment?

I got bitten in the behind by a swear toad once. We were sweeping a tunnel for a rogue troll and the little guy just popped out of a hole and took a chunk out of me. It was a small chunk, but the venom caused a lot of swelling. I will never live that day down. I just hope Artemis Fowl doesn't find out about it.

You often get into trouble with Commander Root for not following the rules. Did you use to get into trouble at school for not following the rules, too?

My father always taught me to do what's right, no matter what the cost. And that's what I do. Rules are important, but the right thing is more important. Sometimes that got me in trouble at school. I can never keep my mouth shut if I see someone being bullied or punished unjustly. It's just the way I am.

What was your favorite subject at school?

I loved virtual school. You get to put on a V-Helmet and travel through history. Those helmets are amazing—they even have special air filters so you can smell the period you are studying.

What do you really think of Artemis Fowl?

I'm of two minds about Artemis. Half of me wants to hug him and the other half wants to throw him in a cell for a few months to teach him a lesson. For all his brains, Artemis does not understand the consequences of his schemes. Every time he sets off on an adventure, someone seems to get hurt. And Butler is not always going to be around to save him. And I'm not always going to be around to save Butler.

What are your hobbies?

I read a lot. Mostly the classics—Horri Antowitz is a good author, and Burger Melviss. I like a good thriller. I also like crunchball and I play in the police league. I'm the second dunker, which can really take it out of a girl.

What is your most treasured possession?

I still have the Recon acorns given to me by Commander Root himself. No matter how many medals and promotions I earn, the first acorns are still the best.

What keeps you awake at night?

Some nights I lie awake and think about what the humans are doing to the planet. And I wonder how long it will be before they find out about us. Some nights, if I'm feeling a bit paranoid, then I swear I can hear human crafts over my head. Digging. Burrowing.

Who is your best friend?

Tough one. I'm going to have to go for two: Foaly and Captain Trouble Kelp. They have both saved my life more than once. And they stuck by me in the bad times, when everyone else had written me off as a failure.

INTERVIEW WITH
BUTLER

What are your three top tips for being a successful bodyguard?

Train hard: there is no substitute for knowledge.
Listen to your sensei: they have the experience that you need.
Be prepared to sacrifice everything for the job.

You are very close to your younger sister, Juliet. Were you pleased that she wanted to follow in your footsteps, and do you think she will make a good bodyguard?

I was hoping that Juliet would pick another profession. Juliet has too much life in her to smother inside a bodyguard's uniform. I think that my little sister may still decide to pick a less dangerous profession, like wrestling.

What is your most treasured possession?

My most treasured possession is etched into my skin. It is a blue diamond tattoo from Madam Ko's Bodyguard Academy. I was the youngest-ever graduate of the academy and this tattoo gives me access to circles most people don't even know exist. It's like carrying a resumé on your arm.

What is your favorite book?

I don't have much time to read. Artemis's schemes keep me on my toes. Mostly I read helicopter manuals and keep an eye on weather reports and current affairs. If I do have a moment to myself, I do enjoy a good romance story. If you tell a soul, I will hunt you down.

What is your happiest childhood memory, and why?

I still treasure the days that I spent as a teenager teaching my baby sister how to do spinning kicks in her sandbox.

What is your favorite song?

I like the Irish band U2. Their song "I Still Haven't Found What I'm Looking For" could have been written for Master Artemis.

What is your favorite film?

I don't like shoot-'em-ups; they remind me too much of real life. I like a good romantic comedy. It takes my mind off the stress of my job. My all-time favorite is *Some Like It Hot*.

Where is your favorite place in the world, and why?

My favorite place in the world is by Master Artemis's side, wherever that might be. One thing I know for sure is that wherever we are, it will not be boring.

Bodyguards have to be very brave. What scares you?

All bodyguards have the same fear: we fear failure. If something were to happen to Artemis, and I could have prevented it, that would haunt me for the rest of my life.

INTERVIEW WITH
MULCH DIGGUMS

Do you ever regret taking up a life of crime?
I don't think of it as crime. I think of it as redistribution of wealth. I am only taking back from the humans what they stole from us in the first place. So, no, I don't regret my criminal past, just getting caught. Anyway, I'm going straight from now on. Honest.

All dwarfs are particularly prone to wind, which could be embarrassing for a Mud Man. What was your most embarrassing moment?
Dwarfs are prone to attacks of wind, which is not embarrassing as such, as it is only natural. However, in my chosen profession, loud bursts of wind can be a bit of a setback. I was almost through to the main hall in the Louvre once when a particularly violent blast set off the motion sensors. They were laughing about that for years in the Atlantis Correctional Facility.

What makes you the happiest?
Dwarfs are never happier than when they are tunneling. As soon as we take that first mouthful of soil, we feel at home and safe. In truth, I think that dwarfs as a species are closer to moles than humans.

What was your proudest moment?
I was very proud of the time when I single-handedly saved Artemis and Holly from certain death at the Eleven Wonders Exhibition in the Lower Elements—but I can't tell you too much about that yet, as I gather the adventure has yet to be released on the surface.

You've got into many scrapes during your adventures with Artemis Fowl. What was your scariest moment?

I must admit to being petrified that time below Fowl Manor when I had just dived into my tunnel and Butler caught me by the ankles. Believe me, an enraged Butler is the last person you want dragging you anywhere. Obviously this happened before we became friends.

What do you really think of Artemis Fowl and Butler?

I like the Irish kid. I really do. We have the same interest: gold. We have worked together on the Fei Fei project, and I can see a long future of cooperation.

Captain Holly Short, Commander Julius Root, or Foaly: who do you like the most and why?

Not Julius, that's for certain. I respect him, yes, but like? I don't think anyone really likes Julius, except his officers—they would all die for him. Heaven knows why. I would have to say that Holly is my favorite. She has saved my hairy rear on a couple of occasions, but it's not just that. Holly is that rarest of creatures—a loyal friend. And you don't come across many of those.

What advice would you give a young dwarf?

Firstly, always chew your rocks before swallowing. They pass through easier that way, and your teeth need the roughage. And secondly, never eat the same dirt twice if you can avoid it.

What is your favorite place above or below the earth, and why?

There is a field in county Kerry in Ireland, where the soil is pure and chemical-free. I like to dig myself a little hole about twenty feet down and listen to the sea crash against the rocks two fields over.

INTERVIEW WITH
FOALY

Which invention are you proudest of?

It's hard to pick just one invention—I have registered more patents than any other fairy in history. If I had to pick one, I would say the time-stop towers: a set of five portable towers that allow the LEP to store the time-stopping abilities of several warlocks in battery form, then generate their own time-stop wherever they need to. Ingenious, if I do say so myself. These little towers have got us out of more than one scrape, including the siege of Fowl Manor.

Who or what inspires you?

I must admit that I often read my own articles in scientific journals and inspire myself. But other than myself, my main inspiration is the pixie Opal Koboi. Opal is criminally insane, but she has a fine grasp of engineering and economics. Her Doubledex wing design revolutionized solo flight, and every time she has made an advance I was spurred on to better it.

What are your top three tips to becoming an inventor?

Invent things that people actually want. Keep your thoughts to yourself until you are ready to patent your invention, and always wear a foil hat to deflect brain-probing rays. Those rays have not been invented yet, but you never know.

What are your hobbies?

When I am not in the lab, I like to read articles about me or to watch video footage of my speeches from scientific conventions. I have lately taken up line dancing.

What is your favorite memory?

I remember the exact moment when my quick thinking put an end to the goblin revolution. If it hadn't been for me, everyone in

Police Plaza would shed their skin twice a year. But was I given a medal? Was there a statue erected in the square? No. There's gratitude for you.

What was your favorite subject at school, besides science?

I always fancied myself as a bit of an artist. I abandoned this dream when my art teacher told me that my landscapes were flatter than an ironed sheet of rice paper. This, I presume, is not a good thing. I was crushed and never picked up a brush again.

What keeps you awake at night?

My ideas keep me awake, and the thought that someone else will patent them before I can. I keep a computer fired up beside my bed in case something comes to me in the half-conscious between waking and sleeping.

Most treasured possession?

I own a collection of foil hats. One for every occasion. I have discovered an artisan, who decorates my hats with clever designs. Last week I noticed two other technicians wearing foil hats. I think I may have started a trend.

Which Mud Man do you most admire?

I admire the Sicilian environmentalist Giovanni Zito. He is one of the few humans who is actually trying to make the world a better place. If the rest of the world adopted his solar wind-farm technology, emissions would be down by seventy percent in ten years. If only Zito had Artemis Fowl's brains.

Who is your best friend?

My best friend under this Earth is the elf Holly Short. We are both workaholics and so do not see as much of each other as we would like, but somehow she always makes time for me, especially when work is getting me down. Whenever I am close to smashing a computer in frustration, I look up and see Holly at my elbow waving a carrot. A special elf.

INTERVIEW WITH
COMMANDER
JULIUS ROOT

Why are you harder on Captain Holly Short than you are on other Recon officers? And why were you so against female officers joining Recon?

I was not against female Recon officers, as such, I was just doubtful that they could make the grade. I'm happy to say that Holly proved me wrong, and now there are six other female candidates for Recon in the pipeline. I was hard on Holly because I had read her psych report, and I knew my attitude would make her more determined to pass the initiation. Naturally, I was right.

What was your proudest moment?

My proudest moment was when Captain Short shut down the goblin rebellion. I had put a lot of faith in that elf, and she didn't let me down.

What makes you laugh out loud?

Nothing. I rarely smile, hardly ever chuckle, and I haven't laughed out loud in 200 years. It's bad for discipline—and if anyone says they have heard me laughing out loud, I want their name and rank.

You and Foaly seem to have a love/hate relationship. What do you really think of him?

Love/hate? Well, you're half right. Most of the time, I want to drop-kick that smug centaur out of my building. But I will admit, grudgingly, that his gadgets do come in useful on occasion. If they didn't, he would be out of a job in a heartbeat.

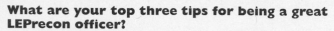

What are your top three tips for being a great LEPrecon officer?

One: listen to your commander—he is always right.

Two: ignore all hunches, unless suggested by your commander, who is always right.

Three: if in doubt, call your commander. The one who is always right.

If you hadn't been an LEP commander, what would you have liked to be?

I always fancied myself as a landscape gardener, or a mime artist. Are you crazy? The LEP is the only job for me. If it didn't exist, I'd have to invent it.

What was your favorite subject at school, and why?

I always liked history, especially military tactics. By the age of six I knew exactly what King Frond should have done at the Battle of Ochre Stew. If I had been his tactician, then maybe his dynasty would have lasted another few centuries.

Trouble Kelp or Holly Short? Who is the better Recon officer in your opinion?

Trouble is more reliable, but Holly is more instinctive. If I were stuck in a diabolical trap, I would want Trouble to find the trap and Holly to get me out of it.

Do you think that Mud Men and fairies could ever live in harmony?

I doubt it. Mud Men can't even live in harmony with themselves. Though I have to admit that our surveillance has revealed a substantial mood swing among the younger generations over the past few years. They are less warlike and more understanding. So maybe there is a glimmer of hope after all.

INTERVIEW WITH
EOIN COLFER

What is your favorite book?
Stig of the Dump.

What is your favorite song?
"The Great Beyond" by REM.

What is your favorite film?
The Silence of the Lambs.

What are your most treasured possessions?
Books.

When did you start writing?
My first attempt at proper writing was way back in sixth grade. I wrote a play for the class about Norse gods. Everyone died in the end except me.

Where do you get your ideas and inspiration from?
Inspiration comes from experience. My imagination is like a cauldron bubbling with all the things I've seen and places I've visited. My brain mixes them all up and regurgitates them in a way that I hope is original.

Can you give your top three tips to becoming a successful author?

1. Practice. Write every day even if it's only for ten minutes. Remember, nothing is wasted. Eventually your style will emerge. Persevere!

2. Don't submit your manuscript until it is as good as you can make it. Edit! Cut! Chop! Trust your editor.

3. Get a good agent. They will find the publisher that is right for you.

What is your favorite memory?

One of my favorite memories is from my wedding day, when my wife and her three sisters lined up for an impromptu Irish dancing session—a precursor to *Riverdance*.

Where is your favorite place in the world and why?

Slade, a small fishing village in Ireland. It's where I spent the holidays of my youth fishing, and now I go back with my own son.

What are your hobbies?

My main hobby is reading: I even read the labels on jars! I also love the theater and have written a few plays. I have recently been introduced to parachuting!

If you hadn't been a writer, what do you think you would have been?

If I hadn't become a writer, I think I would have continued as a primary-school teacher. Kids are a great source of inspiration.

Saint Bartleby's School for Young Gentlemen

Annual Report

Student: Artemis Fowl II
Year: First
Fees: Paid
Tutor: Dr. Po

Language Arts

As far as I can tell, Artemis has made absolutely no progress since the beginning of the year. This is because his abilities are beyond the scope of my experience. He memorizes and understands Shakespeare after a single reading. He finds mistakes in every exercise I administer, and has taken to chuckling gently when I attempt to explain some of the more complex texts. Next year I intend to grant his request and give him a library pass during my class.

Mathematics

Artemis is an infuriating boy. One day he answers all my questions correctly, and the next every answer is wrong. He calls this an example of the chaos theory, and says that he is only trying to prepare me for the real world. He says the notion of infinity is ridiculous. Frankly, I am not trained to deal with a boy like Artemis. Most of my pupils have trouble counting without the aid of their fingers. I am sorry to say, there is nothing I can teach Artemis about mathematics, but someone should teach him some manners.

Social Studies

Artemis distrusts all history texts, because he says history is written by the victors. He prefers living history, where survivors of certain events can actually be interviewed. Obviously this makes studying the Middle Ages somewhat difficult. Artemis has asked for permission to build a time machine next year during our double periods so that the entire class may view medieval Ireland for ourselves. I have granted his wish, and would not be at all surprised if he succeeded in his goal.

Science

Artemis does not see himself as a student, rather as a foil for the theories of science. He insists that the periodic table is a few elements short and that the theory of relativity is all very well on paper but would not hold up in the real world, because space will disintegrate before time. I made the mistake of arguing once, and young Artemis reduced me to near tears in seconds. Artemis has asked for permission to conduct failure analysis tests on the school next term. I must grant his request, as I fear there is nothing he can learn from me.

Social & Personal Development

Artemis is quite perceptive and extremely intellectual. He can answer the questions on any psychological profile perfectly, but this is only because he knows the perfect answers. I fear that Artemis feels that the other boys are too childish. He refuses to socialize, preferring to work on his various projects during free periods. The more he works alone, the more isolated he becomes, and if he does not change his habits soon, he may isolate himself completely from anyone wishing to be his friend, and, ultimately, from his family too. Must try harder.

Fairy Quiz

Follow this simple test to see if you might have fairy ancestry.

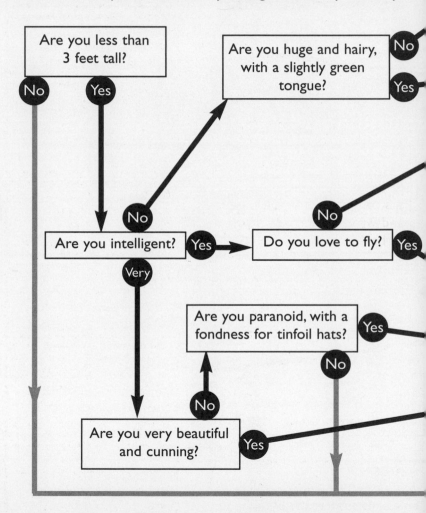

Are you less than 3 feet tall?

No Yes

Are you huge and hairy, with a slightly green tongue?

No Yes

No

Are you intelligent? Yes

Very

Do you love to fly?

No Yes

Are you paranoid, with a fondness for tinfoil hats?

Yes No

No

Are you very beautiful and cunning?

Yes

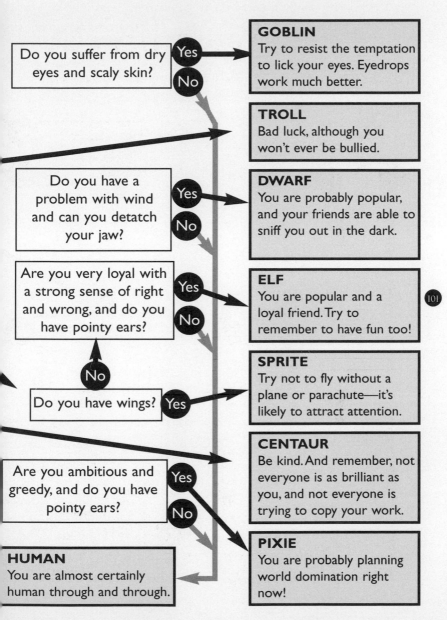

GOBLIN
Try to resist the temptation to lick your eyes. Eyedrops work much better.

Do you suffer from dry eyes and scaly skin? **Yes** / **No**

TROLL
Bad luck, although you won't ever be bullied.

Do you have a problem with wind and can you detatch your jaw? **Yes** / **No**

DWARF
You are probably popular, and your friends are able to sniff you out in the dark.

Are you very loyal with a strong sense of right and wrong, and do you have pointy ears? **Yes** / **No**

ELF
You are popular and a loyal friend. Try to remember to have fun too!

101

No
Do you have wings? **Yes**

SPRITE
Try not to fly without a plane or parachute—it's likely to attract attention.

CENTAUR
Be kind. And remember, not everyone is as brilliant as you, and not everyone is trying to copy your work.

Are you ambitious and greedy, and do you have pointy ears? **Yes** / **No**

HUMAN
You are almost certainly human through and through.

PIXIE
You are probably planning world domination right now!

There are many shuttle ports disguised throughout the world, where fairies come and go among humans. Their locations are closely guarded secrets. So far, Artemis Fowl knows the locations of only a few.

Can you match the shuttle port or chute with the locations below?

A   Tara, Ireland

B   Murmansk, northern Russia

C   Martina Franca, Italy

D   Wajir, Kenya

E   Los Angeles, USA

F   Stonehenge, UK

G   Paris, France

A   B   C

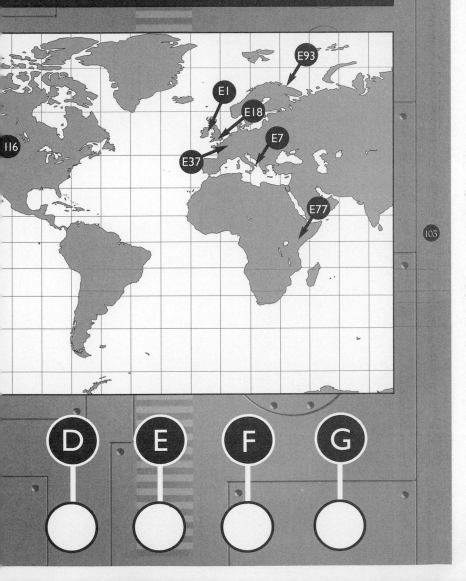

116

103

D   E   F   G

Foaly's Inventions

Titanium pod: capable of carrying LEP officers to the Earth's surface, either powered by its own motor or able to ride on currents of hot gas released by magma flares.

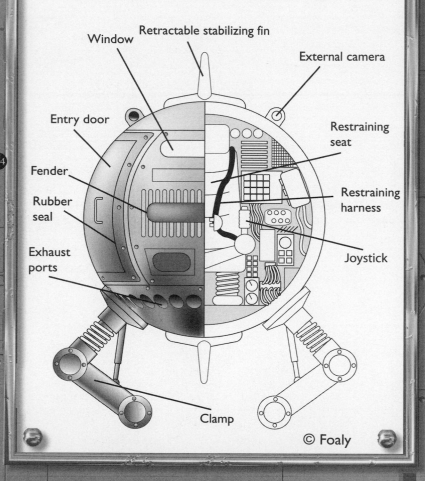

Window

Retractable stabilizing fin

External camera

Entry door

Restraining seat

Fender

Restraining harness

Rubber seal

Joystick

Exhaust ports

Clamp

© Foaly

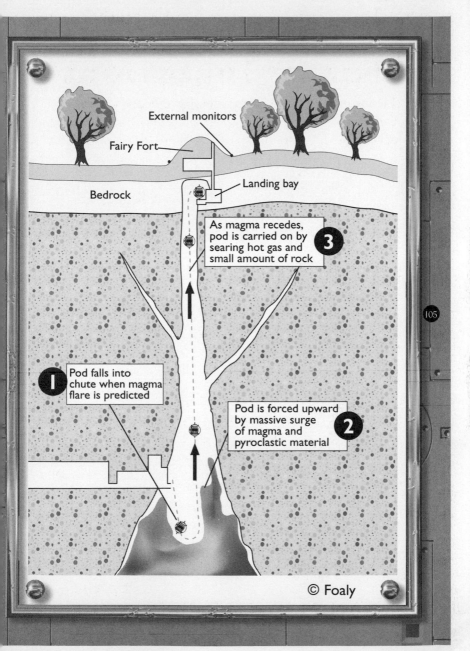

External monitors

Fairy Fort

Bedrock

Landing bay

3 As magma recedes, pod is carried on by searing hot gas and small amount of rock

1 Pod falls into chute when magma flare is predicted

2 Pod is forced upward by massive surge of magma and pyroclastic material

© Foaly

Equipment for a member of the LEP Retrieval Squad

Locator

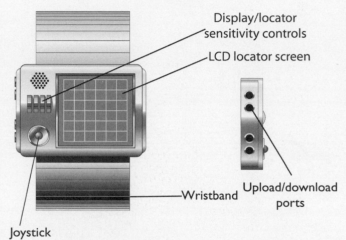

Display/locator sensitivity controls

LCD locator screen

Upload/download ports

Wristband

Joystick

Wings ("Dragonfly" model)

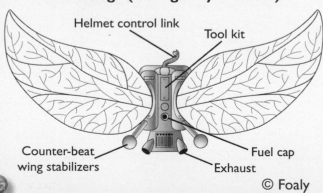

Helmet control link

Tool kit

Counter-beat wing stabilizers

Fuel cap

Exhaust

© Foaly

Helmet

Loudspeakers

Live-feed camera

Ventilation ducts

Visor housing

400-watt lamp

Pressure seal

Oxygen/pollution
mask (detatchable)

Control buttons

Voice-activated microphone

© Foaly

CROSSWORD

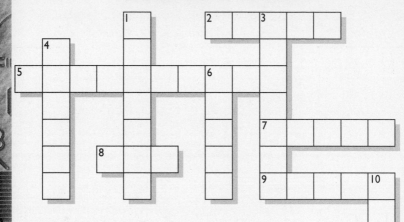

Across

2 Brilliant, but paranoid, inventor

5 Captain Holly Short should have been, but wasn't, when she first met Artemis Fowl

7 Criminal dwarf with a particularly bad wind problem

8 Acronym for the law enforcement officers of the fairy People

9 Surname of the only female LEPrecon officer

11 Titanium egg-shaped vehicles designed to take fairies to the surface of the Earth

12 What Captain Holly Short loves to do, with the aid of Foaly's latest designs

Down

1 Collective name for elves, trolls, pixies, sprites etc....

3 The name shared by the goddess of the hunt and a young criminal mastermind

4 The name that fairies give to humans

6 _____City. The home of the fairy People

10 Probably the most dangerous fairy of all, as Butler found out in *Artemis Fowl*

Fairy Word Search

Find the twelve hidden words. They could be written
forward or backward; and across, up, down, or diagonal.

M	P	T	H	E	R	I	T	U	A	L
I	S	S	T	E	L	G	R	O	O	X
N	W	P	M	L	C	C	O	H	P	R
D	X	X	R	S	O	X	L	Z	V	E
W	I	N	G	I	N	B	L	A	A	L
I	C	V	O	T	T	B	P	N	N	T
P	A	R	L	N	M	E	I	S	C	U
E	L	F	D	A	A	G	M	O	N	B
G	G	O	B	L	I	N	C	T	W	N
I	S	E	G	T	K	N	X	A	X	X
O	W	Q	M	A	Z	C	E	R	R	J
P	O	L	I	C	E	P	L	A	Z	A

109

THE RITUAL   WING   ELF
ATLANTIS   GOBLIN   BUTLER
TROLL   MINDWIPE   SPRITE
POLICE PLAZA   TARA   GOLD

This section of the Lower Elements Police Artemis Fowl *file is sealed and may not be accessed by anyone with less than alpha+ security clearance. The Fei Fei affair occurred shortly after the fairy People's initial contact with Artemis Fowl. At this time, Artemis's mother had been returned to health by LEP Captain Holly Short, but his father was still missing, presumed dead, in northern Russia.*

THE
SEVENTH
DWARF

CHAPTER I: LADY FEI FEI'S TIARA

Below the Fleursheim Plaza, Manhattan, New York City

DWARFS dig tunnels. That's what they are born to do. Their bodies have adapted over millions of years to make them efficient tunnelers. A dwarf male's jaw can be unhinged so that he can unhook it at will in order to excavate a tunnel with his mouth. The waste is jettisoned at the rear end to make way for the next mouthful.

The dwarf that concerns us is the notorious fairy felon Mulch Diggums. Mulch found burglary much more suited to his personality than mining. The hours were shorter, the risks were less severe, and the precious metals and stones that he took from the Mud Men were already processed, forged, and polished.

Tonight's target was the tiara of Lady Fei Fei, a legendary Chinese diplomat. The tiara was a masterpiece of intricate jade-and-diamond arrangements in a white-gold setting. It was priceless, though Mulch would sell it for much less.

The tiara was currently on tour as the centerpiece of an Asian art exhibition. On the evening our story begins, it was overnighting in the Fleursheim Plaza on its way to the Metropolitan Museum. For one night only, Fei Fei's tiara was vulnerable and Mulch did not intend to miss his chance.

Incredibly, the original geological planning survey for the Fleursheim Plaza was freely available on the Internet, allowing Mulch to plot his route from the comfort of the East Village, where he was holed up. The dwarf discovered, to his delight, that a narrow vein of compacted clay and loose shale ran right up to the basement wall. The basement where the Fei Fei tiara was being stored.

At that moment, Mulch was closing his jaws around five pounds of earth per second as he burrowed ever closer to the Fleursheim basement. His hair and beard resembled an electrified halo as each sensitive fiber tested the surface for vibrations.

It wasn't bad clay, Mulch mused as he swallowed, taking shallow breaths through his nostrils. Breathing and swallowing simultaneously is a skill lost by most creatures once they leave infancy, but for dwarfs it is essential for survival.

Mulch's beard hair detected vibration close by; the steady thrumming that usually indicated air-conditioning units or a generator. That didn't necessarily mean he was nearing his target. But Mulch Diggums had the best internal compass in the business, plus he'd programmed the precise coordinates into the stolen Lower Elements Police helmet in his knapsack. Mulch paused long enough to check the 3D grid in the helmet's visor. The Fleursheim basement was forty-eight degrees northeast, ten yards above his present position. A matter of seconds for a tunnel dwarf of his caliber.

Mulch resumed his munching, scything through the clay like a fairy torpedo. He was careful to expel only clay at the lower end, and not air. The air might be needed if he encountered any obstacles. Seconds later he encountered the very barrier he had been saving up for. His skull collided with six inches of basement cement. Dwarf skulls may be tough, but they cannot crack half a foot of concrete.

"D'Arvit!" swore Mulch, blinking concrete flakes from his eyes with long dwarf lashes. He reached up, rapping a knuckle against the flat surface.

"Five or six inches, I reckon," he said to no one, or so he thought. "Should be no problem."

Mulch backed up, compacting the earth behind him. He was about to employ a maneuver known in dwarf culture as the *cyclone*. This move was generally used for emergency escapes or for impressing dwarf females. He jammed the unbreakable LEP helmet over his wild hair, drawing his knees to his chin.

"I wish you could see this, ladies," he muttered, allowing the gas in his insides to build. He had swallowed a lot of air in the past few minutes, and now individual bubbles were merging to form an increasingly difficult-to-contain tube of pressure.

"A few more seconds," grunted Mulch, the pressure bringing a glow to his cheeks.

Mulch crossed his arms over his chest, drew in his beard hair, and released the pent-up wind.

The result was spectacular and would have earned Mulch the girlfriend of his choice, if anyone had been around to see it. If you imagine the tunnel to be the neck of a champagne bottle, then Mulch was the cork. He shot up that passageway at over a hundred miles per hour, spinning like a top. Ordinarily when bone meets concrete, the concrete wins, but Mulch's head was protected by a stolen fairy Lower Elements Police helmet. These helmets are made from a virtually indestructible polymer.

Mulch punched through the basement floor in a flurry of concrete dust and spinning limbs. The dust was whipped into a dozen mini-whirlwinds by his jet stream. His momentum took him a full six feet into the air before he flopped to the floor, and lay there panting. The cyclone took a lot out of a person. Who said crime was easy?

After a quick breather, Mulch sat up and re-hinged his jaw. He would have liked a longer rest but there could be cameras pointed at him right now. There was probably a scrambler on the helmet, but technology had never been his strong point. He needed to nab the tiara, and escape underground.

He stood, shaking a few lumps of clay from his bum flap, and took a quick look around. There were no telltale red lights winking on CCTV cameras. There were no safety-deposit boxes for valuable artifacts. There wasn't even a particularly secure door. It seemed an odd place for a priceless tiara to be stored even for one night. Humans were inclined to protect their treasures, especially from other humans.

Something winked at him from the darkness. Something that gathered in and reflected the minuscule amount of light available in the base-ment. There was a plinth among the statues, storage crates, and mini-skyscrapers of stacked chairs. And atop the plinth was a tiara, and the spectacular blue diamond at its center glittered even in almost total darkness.

Mulch burped in surprise. The Mud Men had left Fei Fei's tiara out in the open? Not likely. This must be a setup.

He approached the plinth cautiously, wary of any traps on the ground. But there was nothing, no motion sensors, no laser eyes. Nothing. Mulch's instinct screamed at him to flee, but his curiosity pulled him toward the tiara like a swordfish on a line.

"Moron," he said to himself, or so he thought. "Get out while you can. Nothing good can come of this." But the tiara was magnificent. Mesmerizing.

Mulch ignored his misgivings about the situation, admiring the jeweled item in front of him.

"Not half bad," he said, or maybe it was. The dwarf leaned closer.

The stones had an unnatural sheen to them. Oily. Not clean like real gems. And the gold was too shiny. Nothing a human eye would notice. But gold is life to a dwarf. It is in their blood and dreams.

Mulch lifted the tiara. It was too light. A tiara of this size should weigh at least two pounds.

There were two possible conclusions to be drawn from all this. Either this was a decoy and the real tiara was safely hidden elsewhere, or this was a test, and he had been lured here to take that test. But lured here by whom? And for what purpose?

These questions were answered almost immediately. A giant Egyptian sarcophagus popped open in the deepest of the shadows, revealing two figures who were most definitely not mummies.

"Congratulations, Mulch Diggums," said the first, a pale boy with dark hair. Mulch noticed that he wore night-vision goggles. The other was a giant bodyguard who Mulch had humiliated recently enough for it to still smart. The man's name was Butler, and he did not look in the best of moods.

"You have passed my test," continued the boy, in confident tones. He straightened his suit jacket and stepped from the sarcophagus, extending a hand.

"A pleasure to meet you. Mister Diggums, I am your new business partner. Allow me to introduce myself. My name is . . ."

Mulch shook the hand. He knew who this boy was. They had battled before, just not face-to-face. He was the only human to ever have stolen fairy gold, and managed to keep it. Whatever he had to say, Mulch was certain that it would be interesting.

"I know who you are, Mud Boy," said the dwarf. "Your name is Artemis Fowl."

CHAPTER 2: HİGH PRİORİTY

Police Plaza, Haven City; The Lower Elements

 WHEN Mulch Diggums said the name *Artemis Fowl*, the Mud Boy's file was automatically shunted to the "hot" pile in Police Plaza. Every fairy Lower Elements Police helmet was fitted with a satellite tracker and could be located anywhere in the world. They also had voice-activated microphones, so whatever Mulch said was heard by a surveillance intern. The case was immediately removed from the intern's desktop when Artemis's name was mentioned. Artemis Fowl was fairy enemy number one, and anything related to the Irish boy was sent immediately to the LEP's technical adviser, the centaur, Foaly.

Foaly listened to the live transmission from Mulch's helmet, and cantered into LEP Commander Root's office.

"We have something here, Julius. It could be important."

Commander Julius Root looked up from the fungus cigar he was clipping. The elf did not look happy, but then he rarely did. His complexion was not as rosy as usual, but the centaur had a feeling that was about to change.

"A few words of advice, pony boy," snapped Root, tearing the tip from the cigar. "One, don't call me Julius. And two, there is a protocol in place for speaking to me. I'm the commander here, not one of your polo buddies."

He leaned back in his chair, lighting the cigar. Foaly was unimpressed by all the posturing.

"Whatever. This is important. Artemis Fowl's name has come in on a sound file."

Root sat up abruptly, protocol forgotten. Less than a year previously Artemis Fowl had kidnapped one of his captains, and extorted half a ton of gold from the LEP ransom fund. But more important than the gold itself was the knowledge inside the Irish boy's head. He knew of the People's existence, and might decide to exploit them again.

"Talk quickly, Foaly. No jargon, just Gnommish."

Foaly sighed. Half the fun of delivering vital news was explaining how his technology had made gathering the news possible.

"Okay. I think Fowl has somehow got hold of an LEP helmet. You know that a certain amount of LEP hardware goes missing every year."

"Which is why we can remote-destruct it."

"In most cases, yes."

The commander's cheeks flushed angrily. "Most cases, Foaly? You never said anything about '*most cases*' during the budget meeting."

Foaly raised his palms. "Hey, you try to remote-destruct this helmet if you like. See what happens."

The commander glared at him suspiciously. "And why shouldn't I just press the button right now?"

"Because the self-destruct has been switched off, meaning someone clever has got hold of it.

Previously the helmet was active, which means someone was wearing it. We couldn't risk blowing off a fairy's head, even if he or she is a criminal."

Root chewed the butt of his cigar. "I'm tempted, believe me. Where did this helmet come from? And who is wearing it?"

Foaly consulted a computer file on the com-card in his palm. "It's an old model. Best guess, a surface fence sold it to a rogue dwarf."

Root crushed the cigar into an ashtray. "Dwarfs. If they're not mining protected areas, they're stealing from the humans. Do we have a name?"

"No. The signal is too weak for us to run a voice-pattern analysis. Anyway, even if we could, as you know, due to the unique positioning of their larynx, all dwarf males have basically the same voice."

"This is all I need," groaned the commander. "Another dwarf on the surface. I thought we'd seen the last of that when . . ." He paused, saddened by a sudden memory. The dwarf Mulch Diggums had been killed months earlier, tunneling out of Artemis Fowl's manor. Mulch had been a huge pain in the rear end, but he hadn't been without charisma.

"So, what do we know?"

Foaly read from a list on his screen. "Our uniden-tified subject burrows into a Manhattan basement, where he meets Artemis Fowl Junior. Then they leave together, so something is definitely up."

"What is up, exactly?"

"We don't know. Fowl knew enough about our technology to turn off the mike, and the self-destruct, probably because Butler took a load of equipment from LEP Retrieval during the Fowl Manor siege."

"What about global positioning? Did Artemis know enough to turn that off?"

Foaly grinned smugly. "That can't be turned off. Those old helmets had a tracker layer sprayed on."

"How fortunate for us. Where are they now?"

"In Fowl's jet, heading for Ireland. It's a Lear, top of the line." Foaly noticed the commander's laser stare. "But you probably don't care about the jet, so let's move on, shall we?"

"Yes, let's," said Root caustically. "Do we have anyone topside?"

Foaly activated a large plasma screen on the wall, quickly negotiating his way through files to a world map. There were fairy icons pulsing in various countries.

"We have three Retrieval teams but nobody in the old country."

"Naturally," groaned Root. "That would be far too handy." He paused. "Where's Captain Short?"

"On vacation aboveground. I would remind you that she's off field duty, pending a tribunal."

Root waggled his fingers at imaginary regulations. "Minor detail. Holly knows Fowl better than any fairy alive. Where is she?"

Foaly consulted his computer, as if he didn't already know. As if he didn't make a dozen calls from his workstation every day, to see if Holly had picked up that hoof moisturizer he'd asked for.

"She's in the Cominetto Spa. I don't know about this, Commander. Holly is tough, but Artemis Fowl kidnapped her. Her judgement could be clouded."

"No," said Root. "Holly is one of my best officers, even if she doesn't believe it. Get me a line to that spa. She's going back to Fowl Manor."

CHAPTER 3: **THE SEVENTH DWARF**

The Island of Cominetto, Off the Coast of Malta,
The Mediterranean

 THE Cominetto Spa is the most exclusive holiday destination for the People. It took several years of repeated application to get visa approval for a visit, but Foaly had done a little computer hocus-pocus to get Holly on the shuttle to the Spa. She needed the break after what she'd been through. And was still going through. For now, instead of giving her a medal for saving half of the ransom fund, LEP Internal Affairs was actually investigating her.

In the past week, Holly had been exfoliated, laser peeled, purged (don't ask), and tweezered within an inch of her life, all in the name of relaxation. Her coffee-colored skin was smooth and blemish free, and her cropped auburn hair glowed with internal luster. But she was bored out of her skull.

The sky was blue, the sea was green, and the living was easy. And Holly knew that she would go completely berserk if she had to spend one more minute being pampered. But Foaly had been so pleased when he had set this trip up that she didn't have the heart to tell him how fed up she was.

Today she was lying in a bubble pool of algae sludge having her pores rejuvenated and playing *Guess the Crime*. This was a game in which you assumed everyone who passed by was a criminal, and you had to guess what they were guilty of.

The white-suited algae therapist wandered over with a phone on a transparent tray.

"A call from Police Plaza, Sister Short," he said. His tone left Holly in no doubt what he thought of phone calls in this oasis of calm.

"Thank you, Brother Hummus," she said, snatching the handset. Foaly was on the other end.

"Bad news, Holly," said the centaur. "You've been recalled to active duty. A special assignment."

"Really?" said Holly, simultaneously punching the air and trying to sound disappointed. "What's the assignment?"

"Take a couple of deep breaths," advised Foaly. "And maybe a few pills."

"What is it, Foaly?" insisted Holly, though her gut already knew.

"It's . . ."

"Artemis Fowl," said Holly. "I'm right, aren't I?"

"Yes," admitted Foaly. "The Irish boy is back. And he's teamed up with a dwarf. We don't know what they're planning, so you need to find out."

Holly clambered from the sludge tub, leaving a trail of green algae on the white carpet.

"I can't imagine what they are planning," she said, bursting into the locker room. "But I can tell you two things. We won't like it, and it won't be legal."

*   *   *

The Fowl Lear Jet, Over the Atlantic Ocean

Mulch Diggums was soaking in the Lear jet's high tech Jacuzzi bath. He absorbed gallons of water through his thirsty pores, flushing the toxins from his system. When he felt sufficiently refreshed, he emerged from the bathroom wrapped in an oversize bathrobe. He looked like nothing more than the world's ugliest bride, trailing a train behind him.

Artemis Fowl was toying with an iced tea while he waited for the dwarf. Butler was flying the plane.

Mulch sat down at the coffee table and poured an entire saucer of nuts down his gullet, shells and all.

"So, Mud Boy," he said. "What's going on in that devious brain of yours?"

Artemis steepled his fingers, peering around them through wide-set blue eyes. There was quite a lot going on in his devious mind, but Mulch Diggums would only be hearing a small portion of it. Artemis did not believe in sharing all the details of his schemes with anyone. Sometimes the success of these plans depended on nobody knowing exactly what they were doing. Nobody but Artemis himself.

Artemis put on his friendliest face, leaning forward in his chair.

"The way I see it, Mulch," he said. "You already owe me a favor."

"Really, Mud Boy? And how do you figure that?"

Artemis patted the LEP helmet on the table beside him. "No doubt you bought this on the black market. It is an older model, but it still has the standard LEP voice-activated mike, and the self-destruct."

Mulch tried to swallow the nuts, but his throat was suddenly dry.

"Self-destruct?"

"Yes. There's enough explosive packed in here to turn your head to jelly. There would be nothing left but teeth. Of course there would be no need to activate the self-destruct if the voice-activated mike leads the LEP right to your door. I have switched these functions off."

Mulch frowned. He would be having words with the fence who had sold him the helmet.

"Okay. Thanks. But you don't expect me to believe that you saved me out of the goodness of your heart."

Artemis chuckled. He could hardly expect anyone who knew him to believe that.

"No. We have a common goal. The Fei Fei tiara."

Mulch folded his arms across his chest. "I work alone. I don't need you to help me steal the tiara."

Artemis plucked a newspaper from the table, spinning it across to the dwarf. "Too late, Mulch. Someone already beat us to it."

The headline was in bold capitals: CHINESE TIARA STOLEN FROM MET.

Mulch frowned. "I'm getting a bit confused here, Mud Boy. The tiara was at the Met? It was supposed to be at the Fleursheim."

Artemis smiled. "No, Mulch. The tiara was never at the Fleursheim. That was just what I needed you to believe."

"How did you know about me?"

"Simple," replied Artemis. "Butler told me of your unique tunneling talents, so I began to research recent robberies. A pattern began to emerge. A series of

jewelery robberies in New York state. All subterranean entries. It was a simple matter to lure you
to the Fleursheim by planting some misinformation
at Arty Facts, the Web site you get your data from.
Obviously, with the special talents you displayed at
Fowl Manor, you would be invaluable to me."

"But now someone else has stolen the tiara."

"Exactly. And I need you to recover it."

Mulch sensed that he had the upper hand. "And
why would I want to recover it? And even if I did,
why would I need you, human?"

"I need precisely *that* tiara, Mulch. The blue
diamond on its crown is unique, in hue and quality. It
will form the basis for a new laser I am developing.
The rest of the tiara will be yours to keep. We would
be a formidable team. I plan, you execute. You will
live out your exile in total luxury. This first job will
be a test."

"And if I say no?"

Artemis sighed. "Then I will post my information
concerning your being alive and your whereabouts
on the Internet. I'm sure LEP Commander Root,

will stumble on it eventually. Then, I fear, your exile will be short-lived and completely devoid of luxury."

Mulch jumped to his feet. "So it's blackmail, is it?"

"Only if it has to be. I prefer 'cooperation.'"

Mulch felt his stomach acid bubble. Root thought he had died during the Fowl Manor siege. If the LEP found out that he was alive, then the commander would make it his personal mission to put Mulch behind bars. He didn't have much choice.

"Okay, human. I'll do this job. But no partnership. One job only, then I disappear. I feel like going straight for a couple of decades."

"Very well. It's a bargain. Remember, if you ever change your mind, there are many so-called impregnable vaults in the world."

"One job," insisted Mulch. "I'm a dwarf. We work alone."

Artemis pulled a sheet of paper from a tube, spreading it on the table.

"That's not strictly true, you know," he said,

pointing to the first column on the sheet. "The tiara was stolen by dwarfs, and they have been working together for several years. Very successfully, too."

Mulch crossed the room, reading the name above Artemis's finger.

"Sergei the Significant," he said. "I think someone has an inferiority complex."

"He's the leader. There are six dwarfs in Sergei's little band, collectively known as the Significants," continued Artemis. "You are to be the seventh."

Mulch giggled hysterically. "Of course, why not? The seven dwarfs. This day started off badly, and my beard hair tells me that it's about to get a whole lot worse."

Butler spoke for the first time. "If I were you, Mulch," he said in his deep gravelly tones, "I'd trust the hair."

Holly was out of the spa as soon as she had hosed the algae from her skin. She could have taken a shuttle back to Haven, then caught a connecting flight, but Holly preferred to fly.

Foaly contacted her on her helmet intercom as she skipped across the Mediterranean wave tops, trailing her fingers in the spume.

"Hey, Holly, did you get that hoof cream?"

Holly smiled. No matter what the crisis, Foaly never lost sight of his first priority: himself. She dipped the flaps on her wings, rising to a hundred feet.

"Yes, I got it. It's being couriered down. There was a buy-one-get-one-free deal on. So expect two tubs."

"Excellent. You have no idea how hard it is to get good moisturizer below ground. Remember, Holly, this is between us. The rest of the guys are still a bit old fashioned when it comes to cosmetics."

"Our little secret," said Holly reassuringly. "Now, do we have any idea yet what Artemis is up to?"

Holly's cheeks reddened at the mere mention of the Mud Boy's name. He had kidnapped her, drugged her, and ransomed her for gold. And just because he'd had a change of heart at the last minute, and decided to let her go, didn't mean all was forgiven.

"We don't know exactly what's going on,"

admitted Foaly. "All we know is that they must be up to no good."

"Any video?"

"Nope. Audio only. And we don't even have that anymore. Fowl must have disconnected the mike. All we have left is the tracker."

"What are my orders?"

"The commander says to stick close, plant a bug if you can, but under no circumstances make contact. That is Retrieval's job."

"Okay. Understood. Surveillance only, no contact with the Mud Boy or the dwarf."

Foaly opened a video window in Holly's visor, so she could see the skepticism on his face. "You say that as if the very idea of disobeying an order is unheard of for you. If I remember correctly, and I think I do, you've been reported a dozen times for ignoring your superiors."

"I wasn't ignoring them," retorted Holly. "I was taking their opinions under advisement. Sometimes only the officer on the spot can take the proper decision. That's what being a field agent is all about."

Foaly shrugged. "Whatever you say, captain. But if I were you, I'd think twice before going against Julius on this one. He had that look on his face. You know the one."

Holly terminated the link with Police Plaza. Foaly didn't need to explain further. She knew the one.

CHAPTER 4: SHOWTIME

The Circus Maximus; Wexford Racecourse,
Southern Ireland

 ARtemis, Butler and Mulch had ringside seats for the Circus Maximus. This was one of a new breed of circus in which the acts lived up to the advertising, and there were no animals involved. The clowns were genuinely funny, the acrobats were little short of miraculous, and the dwarfs were little and short.

Sergei the Significant and four of his five teammates were lined up at the center of the ring, doing a spot of preshow posturing to the capacity crowd. Each dwarf was less than three feet tall and wore a tight-fitting crimson leotard with a lightning-flash logo. Their faces were concealed by matching masks.

Mulch was wrapped in an oversize raincoat. He wore a peaked hat pulled over his brow, and his face was slathered with a pungent homemade sunblock. Dwarfs are extremely photosensitive, with a burn time of mere minutes, even in overcast conditions.

Mulch poured an entire jumbo carton of popcorn down his gullet.

"Yep," he mumbled, spitting out kernels. "These boys are actual dwarfs, no doubt about it."

Artemis smiled tightly, glad to have his suspicions confirmed. "I discovered them quite by accident. They use the same Web site you do."

"My computer search revealed two patterns, and it was easy to match the circus's movements to a series of crimes. I am surprised that Interpol and the FBI aren't already on to Sergei and his gang. When the Fei Fei tiara's tour schedule was announced, and it coincided with the circus tour, I knew it was no coincidence. I was, of course, correct. The dwarfs stole the tiara, then smuggled it back to Ireland using the circus as cover. Actually it will be far easier to steal the tiara from these dwarfs, than it would have been from the Met."

"And why is that?" asked Mulch.

"Because they are not expecting it," explained Artemis.

Sergei the Significant and his troupe prepared for their first trick. It was as simple as it was impressive. A small unadorned wooden box was lowered by crane into the center of the ring. Sergei, with much bowing and flexing of his tiny muscles, made his way toward the box. He lifted the lid and climbed in. The cynical audience waited for some curtain or screen shenanigans that would allow the little man to escape, but nothing happened. The box sat there. Immobile. With every eye in the tent drilling into its surface. Nobody went within twenty feet of it.

A full minute passed before a second dwarf entered the ring. He set an old fashioned T-bar detonator on the ground and, following a five-second drum roll, pushed the plunger. The box exploded in a dramatic cloud of soot and balsawood. Either Sergei was dead, or he was gone.

"Hmmph," grunted Mulch, amid the thunderous applause. "Not much of a trick."

"Not when you know how it's done," agreed Artemis.

"He gets in the box, he tunnels out to the dressing room, and presumably he shows up again later."

"Correct. They set down another box at the end of the performance, and lo-and-behold, Sergei reappears. It's a miracle."

"Some miracle. All the talents we have, and that's the best those bums could come up with."

Artemis rose. Butler instantly stood behind him to block any possible attack from the rear. "Come, Mister Diggums, we need to plan for tonight."

Mulch swallowed the last of the popcorn. "Tonight? What's tonight?"

"Why, the late-evening performance," replied Artemis with a grin. "And you, my friend, are the star performer."

Fowl Manor, North County Dublin; Ireland

It was a two-hour drive back to Fowl Manor from Wexford. Artemis's mother was waiting for them at the front doors.

"And how was the circus, Arty?" she said, smiling for her boy, in spite of the pain in her eyes. That pain was never far away, not even since the fairy Holly Short had cured her of her depression following the disappearance of her husband, Artemis's father.

"It was fine, Mother. Wonderful, in fact. I asked Mister Diggums here for dinner. He is one of the performers and a fascinating fellow. I hope you don't mind."

"Of course not. Mister Diggums, make the house your own."

"It wouldn't be the first time," muttered Butler under his breath. He escorted Mulch through to the kitchen while Artemis lingered to talk with his mother.

"How are you, Arty, really?"

Artemis did not know how to respond. What was he to say? I am determined to follow in my father's criminal footsteps, because that is what I do best.

Because that is the only way to raise enough money to pay the numerous private detective agencies and Internet search companies that I have employed to find him. But the crimes don't make me happy. Victory is never as sweet as I think it will be.

"I am fine, Mother, really," he said eventually, without conviction.

Angeline hugged him close. Artemis could smell her perfume and feel her warmth.

"You're a good boy," she sighed. "A good son."

The elegant lady straightened. "Now, why don't you go and talk to your new friend. You must have a lot to discuss."

"Yes, Mother," said Artemis, his resolve over-coming the sadness in his heart. "We have a lot to discuss before tonight's show."

The Circus Maximus

Mulch Diggums had cleared himself a hole just below the dwarfs' tent and was waiting to spring into action. They had returned to Wexford for the late-night performance. Early enough for him to dig his way under the tent from an adjacent field. Artemis was inside the main tent right now keeping a close eye on Sergei the Significant and his team. Butler was hanging back by the rendezvous point, waiting for Mulch's return.

Artemis's scheme had seemed plausible back in Fowl Manor. It had even seemed likely that they could get away with it. But now, with the circus vibrations beating down on his head, Mulch could see a slight problem. The problem being that he was putting his neck on the line, while Mud Boy was sitting in a comfy ringside seat eating cotton candy.

Artemis had explained his scheme in Fowl Manor's drawing room.

"I have been keeping close tabs on Sergei and his troupe ever since I discovered their little outfit. They are a canny group. Perhaps it would be easier to steal the gem from whoever they sell the stone on to, but soon the school holidays will be over, and I will be forced to suspend my operations, so I need the blue diamond now."

"For your laser thing?"

Artemis coughed into his hand. "Laser. Yes, that's correct."

"And it has to be this diamond?"

"Absolutely. The Fei Fei blue diamond is unique. Its precise hue makes it one of a kind."

"And that's important, is it?"

"Vital, for light diffraction. It's technical. You wouldn't understand it."

"Hmm," droned Mulch, suspecting that something was being held back. "So how do you propose we get this vital blue diamond?"

Artemis pulled down a projection screen. There was a diagram of the Circus Maximus taped to the surface.

"Here is the circus ring," he said, pointing with a telescopic pointer.

"What? That round thing, with the word ring in the middle? You don't say."

Artemis closed his eyes, breathing deeply. He was unaccustomed to interruptions. Butler tapped Mulch on the shoulder.

"Listen, little man," he advised in his most serious voice. "Or I might remember that I owe you an ignominious beating, like the one you gave me."

Mulch swallowed. "Listen, yes, good idea. Do continue, Mud Boy . . . uh, Artemis."

"Thank you," said Artemis. "Now. We have been observing the dwarf troupe for months, and in all that time they have never left their own tent unguarded, so we presume that this is where they keep their loot. Generally the entire group is there, except during a performance, when five of the six are needed for the acrobatic routine. Our only window of opportunity is during this period when all but one of the dwarfs are in the ring."

"All but one?" enquired Mulch. "I can't be seen by anybody. If they so much as catch a glimpse of me, they'll hunt me down forever. Dwarfs really hold a grudge."

"Let me finish," said Artemis. "I have put some thought into this, you know. We managed to obtain some video one evening in Brussels from a pencil camera that Butler poked through the canvas."

Butler turned on a flat-screen television and pressed PLAY on a video remote. The picture that appeared was gray and grainy, but perfectly recognizable. It showed a single dwarf in a round tent, lounging in a leather armchair. He was dressed in the Significants' leotard and mask and was blowing bubbles through a small wand.

The earthen floor began to vibrate slightly in the center of the tent where the ground looked disturbed, as though a small earthquake were disrupting that spot only. Moments later a three-foot-diameter circle of earth collapsed entirely, and a masked Sergei emerged from the hole. He vented some gas, and gave his comrade the thumbs-up. The bubble-blowing dwarf immediately ran out of the tent.

"Sergei has just tunneled out of his box, and our bubble-blowing friend is needed in the ring," explained Artemis. "Sergei takes over guard duty until the end of the act, when all the other dwarfs return and Sergei reappears in the new box. We have approximately seven minutes to find the tiara."

Mulch decided to pick a few holes in the plan. "How do we know the tiara is even there?"

Artemis was ready for that question. "Because my sources tell me that there are five European jewelery fences coming to tonight's show. They are hardly here to see the clowns."

Mulch nodded slowly. He knew *where* the tiara would be. Sergei and his significant friends would hide everything a few yards below their tent, safely buried beyond the reach of humans. That still left hundreds of square yards to search.

"I'll never find it," he pronounced eventually. "Not in seven minutes."

Artemis opened his laptop. "This is a computer simulation. You are the blue figure. Sergei is the red figure."

On screen the two computer creatures burrowed through simulated earth.

Mulch watched the blue figure for over a minute.

"I have to admit it, Mud Boy," said the dwarf. "It's clever. But I need a tank of compressed air."

Artemis was puzzled. "Air? I thought you could breathe underground."

"I can." The dwarf grinned hugely at Artemis. "It's not for me."

So now Mulch sat in his underground hole with a diver's tank of air strapped to his back. He squatted absolutely silently. Once Sergei entered the earth, his beard hair would be sensitive to the slightest vibration, including radio transmissions, so Artemis had insisted on radio silence until they were in phase two of the plan.

To the west, one high-frequency vibration punched through the ambient noise. Sergei was making his move. Mulch could feel his brother dwarf scything through the earth, possibly toward his secret cache of stolen jewelery.

Mulch concentrated on Sergei's progress. He was tunneling east, but on a downward tangent, obviously heading directly for something. The sonar in Mulch's beard hair fed him constant speed and direction updates. The second dwarf proceeded at a steady pace and incline for almost a hundred yards, then stopped dead. He was checking something. He hoped it was the tiara.

Following half a minute of minimal movement, Sergei made for the surface, almost directly for Mulch. Mulch felt a sheen of sweat coat his back. This was the dangerous part. He reached slowly into his leotard, pulling out a ball the size and color of an orange. The ball was an organic sedative used by Chilean natives. Artemis had assured Mulch that it had no side effects, and would actually clear up any sinus problems Sergei might have.

With infinite care, Mulch positioned himself as close to Sergei's trajectory as he dared, then wiggled the fist containing the sedative ball into the earth. Seconds later, Sergei's scything jaws consumed the ball along with a few pounds of earth. Before he had taken half a dozen bites, his forward motion slowed to a dead halt, and his chewing grew sluggish. Now was the dangerous time for Sergei. If he were left unconscious with a gut full of clay, he could choke. Mulch ate through the thin layer of earth separating them, he flipped the sleeping dwarf onto his back, feeding an air tube deep into the black depths of his cavernous mouth. Once the tube was in place, he twisted the tank's nozzle, sending a sustained jet of air through Sergei's system. The air stream ballooned the little fairy's internal organs, flushing all traces of clay through his system. His body shook as though connected to a live wire, but he did not awaken. Instead he snored on.

Mulch left Sergei curled in the earth, and aimed his chomping jaws toward the surface. The clay was typical Irish, soft and moist, with low-level pollution, and teeming with insect life. Seconds later, he felt his questing fingers break the surface, cool air brushing across their tips. Mulch made sure that the circus mask covered the upper half of his face, then pushed his head aboveground.

There was another dwarf sitting in the armchair. Today he was playing with four yo-yos. One spinning from each hand and each foot. Mulch said nothing, though he felt a sudden longing to chat with his fellow dwarf. He simply gave a thumbs-up signal.

The second dwarf coiled in his yo-yos wordlessly, then, pulling on a pair of pointy toed boots, bolted for the tent flap. Mulch could hear the sudden roar of the crowd as Sergei's box exploded. Two minutes gone. Five minutes left.

Mulch upended his rear and plotted a course for the exact spot where Sergei had stopped. This was not as difficult as it would seem. Dwarfs' internal compasses are fantastic instruments, and can lead the fairy creatures with the same accuracy as any GPS system. Mulch dived.

There was a small chamber hollowed out below the tent. A typical dwarf hidey-hole, with spit-slickened walls providing low-level luminescence in the darkness. Dwarf spit is a multifunctional secretion. Apart from the normal uses, it also hardens on prolonged contact with air to form a lacquer that is not only tough but also slightly luminous.

Sitting in the center of the small chamber was a wooden chest. It was not locked. Why would it be? There would be no one down here but dwarfs. Mulch felt a stab of shame. It was one thing robbing from the Mud Men, but he was ripping off brother dwarfs who were just trying to make an honest living stealing from humans. This was an all-time low. Mulch made up his mind to somehow reimburse Sergei the Significant and his band once the job was over.

The tiara was inside the chest, the blue stone on its crown winking in the light of the spittle. Now there was a real jewel. Nothing fake about that. Mulch stuffed it inside his leotard. There were plenty of other jewels in the box, but he ignored them. It was bad enough taking the tiara. Now all he had to do was haul Sergei to the surface, where he could recover safely, and leave the same way he had come. He would be gone before the other dwarfs realized anything was wrong.

Mulch headed back toward Sergei, collected his limp form and ate his way back to the surface, dragging his sleeping brother dwarf behind him. He rehinged his jaw, climbing from the hole.

The tent was still deserted. The Significants should be well over halfway through their act by now. Mulch dragged Sergei to the lip of the hole, and took a dwarf flint dagger from his boot. He would cut some strips from the chair and secure Sergei's hands, feet and jaws. Artemis had assured him that Sergei would not wake up, but what did the Mud Boy know about dwarf insides?

"Sorry about this, brother," he whispered almost fondly. "I hate to do it, but the Mud Boy has me over a barrel."

Something shimmered in the corner of Mulch's vision. It shimmered and then spoke.

"First I want you to tell me about the Mud Boy, dwarf," it said. "And then I want you to tell me about the barrel."

CHAPTER 5: RINGMASTER

Over the Italian Coast

 HOLLY Short flew north until she came to mainland Italy, then turned forty degrees to the left over the lights of Brindisi.

"You are supposed to avoid major flight routes and city areas," Foaly reminded her over the helmet speakers. "That is the first rule of Recon."

"The first rule of Recon is to find the rogue fairy," Holly retorted. "Do you want me to locate this dwarf or not? If I stick to the coastline, it will take me all night to reach Ireland. My way, I'll get there by eleven P.M. local time. Anyway, I'm shielded."

Fairies have the power to increase their heart rate

and pump their arteries to bursting, which causes their bodies to vibrate so quickly that they are never in one place long enough to be seen. The only human ever to see through this magical trick, pardon the pun, was, of course, Artemis Fowl, who had filmed fairies on a high-speed camera and then viewed the frames still by still.

"Shielding isn't as foolproof as it used to be," noted Foaly. "I have sent the helmet's tracker pattern to your helmet. All you have to do is follow the beep. When you find our dwarf, the commander wants you to . . ."

The centaur's voice faded out in a liquid hiss of static. The magma flares beneath the earth's crust were up tonight, whiting out LEP communications. This was the third flare since she started her journey. All she could do was proceed according to plan, and hope the channels cleared up.

It was a fine night, so Holly navigated using the stars. Of course her helmet had a built-in GPS unit triangulated by three satellites, but stellar navigation was one of the first courses taught in the

LEP academy. It was possible that a Recon officer could be trapped aboveground without science, and under those circumstances the stars could be that officer's only hope of finding a fairy shuttle port.

The landscape sped by below her, dotted by an ever growing number of human enclaves. Each time she ventured topside, there were more. Soon there would be no countryside left, and no trees to make the oxygen. Then everyone would be breathing artificial air aboveground and below it.

Holly tried to ignore the pollution-alert logo flashing in her visor. The helmet would filter out most of it, and anyway she had no choice. It was either fly over the cities, or possibly lose the rogue dwarf. And Captain Holly Short did not like to lose.

She enlarged the search grid in her helmet visor, and zeroed in on a large, circular, striped tent. A circus. The dwarf was hiding in a circus. Hardly original, but an effective place to pose as a human dwarf.

Holly dipped the flaps on her mechanical wings, descending to twenty feet. The tracker beep pulled her off to the left, away from the main tent itself, toward a smaller adjacent one. Holly swooped lower still, making sure to keep her shield fully buzzed up since the area was teeming with humans.

She hovered above the tip of the tent pole. The stolen helmet was inside, no doubt about it. To investigate further, she would have to enter the structure. The fairy bible, or Book, prevented fairies from entering human dwellings uninvited, but recently the high court had ruled that tents were temporary structures and as such were not included in the Book's edict. Holly burned the stitches on the tent's seam with a laser burst from her Neutrino 2000, and slipped inside.

On the earthen surface below were two dwarfs. One had the stolen helmet strapped across his back, the second was jammed down a hole in the ground. Both wore upper face masks and matching red leotards. Very fetching.

This was a surprising development. Dwarfs generally stuck together, yet these two seemed to be playing for different teams. The first appeared to have incapacitated the second, and perhaps was about to go even further. There was a glittering flint dagger in his hand. And dwarfs did not generally draw their weapons unless they intended to use them.

Holly toggled the mike switch on her glove. "Foaly? Come in, Foaly? I have a possible emergency here."

Nothing. White noise. Not even ghost voices. Typical. The most advanced communications system in this galaxy, and possibly a few others, all rendered useless by a few magma flares.

"I need to make contact, Foaly. If you can record this, I have a crime in process, possibly murder. Two fairies are involved. There is no time to wait for Retrieval. I'm going in. Send Retrieval immediately."

Holly's good sense groaned. She was already technically off active duty, so making contact would bury her Recon career for certain. But ultimately that didn't matter. She had joined the LEP to protect the People, and that was exactly what she intended to do.

She set her wings to descend, floating down from the tent shadows.

The dwarf was talking, in that curious gravelly voice common to all male dwarfs.

"Sorry about this, brother," he said, perhaps making excuses for the impending violence. "I hate to do it, but the Mud Boy has me over a barrel."

Enough, thought Holly. There will be no murder here today. She unshielded, speckling into view in a fairy-shaped starburst. "First I want you to tell me about the Mud Boy, dwarf" she said. "And then I want you to tell me about the barrel."

Mulch Diggums recognized Holly immediately. They had met only months previously in Fowl Manor. Funny how some people were fated to meet over and over. To be part of one another's lives.

He dropped both the dagger and Sergei, raising empty palms. Sergei slid back down the hole.

"I know what this looks like, Ho—officer. I was just going to tie him up, for his own good. He had a tunnel convulsion, that's all. He could hurt himself."

Mulch congratulated himself silently. It was a good lie and he had bitten his tongue before he could utter Holly's name. The LEP thought he had died in a cave, and she would not recognize him with the mask on. All Holly could see was silk and beard.

"A tunnel convulsion? Dwarf kids get those, not experienced diggers."

Mulch shrugged. "I'm always telling him. Chew your food. But will he listen? He's a grown dwarf, what can I do? I shouldn't leave him down there, by the way." The dwarf put one foot into the tunnel.

Holly touched down. "One more step, dwarf," she warned. "For now, tell me about the Mud Boy."

Mulch attempted an innocent smile. There was more chance of a great white shark pulling it off. "What Mud Boy, officer?"

"Artemis Fowl," snapped Holly. "Start talking. You're going to jail, dwarf. For how long depends on you."

Mulch chewed it over for a moment. He could feel the Fei Fei tiara pricking his skin beneath the leotard. It had slipped around the side, below the armpit, most uncomfortable. He had a choice to make. Try to complete the job, or look after number one. Fowl or a reduced sentence. It took less than a second to decide.

"Artemis wants me to steal the Fei Fei tiara for him. My . . . ah . . . circus mates had already taken it, and he bribed me to pass it on to him."

"Where is this tiara?"

Mulch reached inside his leotard.

"Slowly, dwarf."

"Okay. Two fingers."

Mulch drew the tiara from under his armpit.

"You don't take bribes I suppose?"

"Correct. This tiara goes back near enough to wherever it came from. Police will get an anonymous tip and find it in a skip."

Mulch sighed. "The old skip routine. Don't the LEP ever get tired of that?"

Holly did not want to be drawn into conversation.

"Toss it on the ground," she instructed. "Then get

down there yourself. Lie on your back."

One did not order a dwarf to lie on the ground on his belly. One click of the jaws, and the perpetrator would be gone in a cloud of dust.

"On my back? That's really uncomfortable with this helmet."

"On your back!"

Mulch obeyed, dropping the tiara and shifting the helmet to the front. The dwarf was thinking furiously. How much time had gone by? Surely the Significants would be back any second. They would come running to relieve Sergei.

"Officer, you really should get out of here."

Holly searched him for weapons. She unstrapped the LEP helmet, rolling it across the floor.

"And why is that?"

"My teammates will be here any second. We're on a tight schedule."

Holly smiled grimly. "Don't worry about it. I can handle dwarfs. My gun has a nuclear battery."

Mulch swallowed, glancing through Holly's legs toward the tent flaps. The Significants had arrived right on time, and three were sneaking through the tent flap, making less noise than ants in slippers. Each dwarf held a flint dagger in his stubby fingers. Mulch heard a rustling overhead, and looked up to see another Significant peering through a fresh rip in the tent seam. Still one unaccounted for.

"The battery isn't important," said Mulch. "It's not how many bullets you have, it's how fast you can shoot."

Artemis was not enjoying the circus. Butler should have contacted him over a minute ago to confirm that Mulch had arrived at the rendezvous point. Something must be wrong. His instinct told him to take a look, but he ignored it. Stick to the plan. Give Mulch every possible second.

The last few seconds ran out moments later when the five dwarfs in the ring took their bows. They exited the ring with a series of elaborate tumbles, and headed for their own tent.

Artemis raised his right fist to his mouth. Strapped across his palm was a tiny microphone, of the type used by the U.S. secret service. A skin-tone earpiece was lodged in his right ear.

"Butler," he said softly—the mike was whisper sensitive. "The Significants have left the building. We must execute plan B."

"Roger," said Butler's voice in his ear.

Of course there was a plan B. Plan A may have been perfect, but the dwarf executing it certainly wasn't. Plan B involved chaos and escape, hopefully with the Fei Fei tiara. Artemis hurried along his row while the second box was lowered into the center of the ring. All around him, children and their parents cooed at the melodrama unfolding before them, unaware of the very real drama that was being played out not twenty yards away.

Artemis approached the dwarfs' tent, sticking to the shadows.

The Significants trotted ahead of him in a group. In seconds they would enter the tent and find that things were not as they should be. There would be delays and confusion, in which time the jewel merchants in the big top would probably come running,

along with their armed security. This mission would have to be either completed or aborted in the next few seconds.

Artemis heard voices from inside the tent. The Significants heard them too and froze. There shouldn't be voices. Sergei was alone, and if he was not, something was wrong. One dwarf crawled on his belly to the flap, peeking inside. Whatever he saw obviously upset him, because he crawled rapidly back to the group, and began issuing frantic instructions. Three dwarfs went in the front flap, one scaled the tent wall, and the other popped his bum flap and went subterranean.

Artemis waited a couple of heartbeats, then crept to the tent flap. If Mulch was still in there, something would have to be done to get him out, even if it meant sacrificing the diamond. He flattened his body against the tightly drawn canvas and peered inside. He was surprised by what he saw. Surprised, but not amazed: he should have expected it, really. Holly Short was standing over a fallen dwarf who may or may not have been Mulch Diggums. The

Significants were closing in on her, daggers drawn.

Artemis raised the radio to his mouth.

"Butler, how far away are you, exactly?"

Butler answered immediately. "I'm on the circus perimeter. Forty seconds, no more."

In forty seconds, Holly and Mulch would be dead. He could not allow that.

"I have to go in," he said tersely. "When you get here, moderate plan B as necessary."

Butler did not waste time arguing. "Roger. Keep them talking, Artemis. Promise them the world, and everything under it. Their greed will keep you alive."

"Understood," said Artemis, stepping into the tent.

"Well, well, well," said Derph, Sergei's second in command. "Looks like the law finally tracked us down."

Holly planted a foot on Mulch's chest, pinning him to the earth. She trained her weapon on Derph.

"That's right, I'm with Recon. Retrieval are

seconds away. So just accept it and lie on your backs."

Derph casually tossed his dagger from hand to hand. "I don't think so, elf. We've been living this life for five hundred years, and we don't plan to stop now. You just let Sergei go, and we'll be on our way. No need for anyone to get hurt."

Mulch realized that the other dwarfs believed he was Sergei. Maybe there was still a way out.

"Just stay where you are," Holly ordered with more bravado than she felt. "It's guns against knives here, you can't possibly win."

Derph smiled through his beard. "We've already won," he said.

With the kind of synchronization born of centuries of teamwork, the dwarfs attacked together. One dropped from the shadows in the tent's upper regions, while another breached the earthen flooring, jaws wide, tunnel wind driving him a full three feet into the air. The vibration of Holly's voice had drawn him to her, as a struggling swimmer's kicks will draw a shark.

"Look out!" screeched Mulch, unwilling to let the Significants deal with Holly, even at the price of his own freedom. He might be a thief, but he realized that that was as low as he was willing to go.

Holly looked up, squeezing off a shot that stunned the descending dwarf, but she did not have time to look down. The second attacker clamped his fingers around her gun, almost taking her hand with it, then wrapped his powerful arms around Holly's shoulders, squeezing the air from her body. The others closed in.

Mulch hopped to his feet.

"Wait, brothers. We need to interrogate the elf, find out what the LEP know."

Derph didn't agree. "No, Sergei. We do as we always do. Bury the witness and move on. Nobody can catch us underground. We take the jewels and go."

Mulch punched the bear-hugging dwarf under the arm, a nerve cluster for dwarfs. He released Holly, and she fell gasping to the earth.

"No," he barked. "I am the pack leader here!

This is an LEP officer. We kill her and a thousand more will be on our trail. We bind her and leave."

Derph tensed suddenly, leveling the tip of his dagger at Mulch. "You are different, Sergei. All this talk of sparing elves. Let me see you without the mask."

Mulch backed up a step. "What are you saying? You can see my face later."

"The mask! Now! Or I'll see your innards as well as your face."

And suddenly Artemis was in the tent, striding across the floor as if he owned the space.

"What is going on here?" he demanded, his accent decidedly German.

All faces turned to him. He was magnetic.

"Who are you?" asked Derph.

Artemis snorted. "Who am I? the little man asks. Did you not invite my master here from Berlin? My name is not important. All you need to know is that I represent Herr Ehrich Stern."

"H–H–Herr Stern, of course," stammered Derph. Ehrich Stern was a legend in the field of precious stones and how to dispose of them illegally. He also disposed of people who disappointed him. He had been invited to the tiara's auction and was sitting in row three, as Artemis well knew.

"We come here to do business, and instead of professionalism we find some kind of dwarf feud."

"There is no feud," said Mulch, still playing the part of Sergei. "Just a little misunderstanding. We are deciding how to dispose of an unwelcome guest."

Again, Artemis snorted. "There is only one way to dispose of unwanted guests. As a special favor, we will perform that service for you, for a discount on the tiara, of course." He paused in disbelief, his eyes widening. "Tell me this is not she," he said, picking the tiara off the ground where Holly had dropped it. "She lies in the dirt like some cluster of common stones. This truly is a circus."

"Hey, take it easy," said Mulch.

"And what is this?" demanded Artemis, pointing to Mulch's helmet in the dirt.

"I dunno," said Derph. "It's an LEP . . . I mean, the intruder's helmet. It's her helmet."

Artemis waggled a finger. "I think not, unless your tiny intruder has two heads. She is already wearing a helmet."

Derph did the maths. "Hey, that's right. So where did that helmet come from?"

Artemis shrugged. "I just got here, but I would guess that you have a traitor in your midst."

The dwarfs turned, as one, toward Mulch.

"The mask!" growled Derph. "Take it off! Now!"

Mulch shot Artemis a look through the mask's eyeholes. "Thanks a bunch."

The dwarfs advanced in a semicircle, knives raised.

Artemis stepped in front of the group. "Halt, little men," he said imperiously. "There is only one way to save this operation, and that is certainly not by staining the earth with blood. Leave these two to my bodyguard, and then we shall commence negotiations."

Derph smelled a rat. "Wait a minute. How do we know you're with Stern? You waltz in here just in time to save these two. It's all a bit convenient if you ask me."

"That's why nobody asks you," retorted Artemis. "Because you're a dullard."

Derph's dagger glittered dangerously. "I've had it with you, kid. I say we get rid of *all* witnesses and move on."

"Fine," said Artemis. "This charade is beginning to bore me." He raised his palm to his mouth. "Time for plan B."

Outside the tent, Butler wrapped the tent's mainstay around his wrist and pulled. He was a man of prodigious strength, and soon the metal pegs began to slide from the mud that held them. The canvas cracked, rippling and ripping. The dwarfs gaped at the billowing canvas.

"The sky is falling," screamed a particularly dense one.

Holly took advantage of the sudden confusion, grabbing a stun grenade on her belt. She had seconds left before the dwarfs cut their losses and went subterranean. Once that happened it was all over. No one could catch a dwarf below ground. By the time Retrieval got here, the dwarfs would be miles away.

The grenade was a strobe that sent out flashing light at such high frequency that too many messages were sent simultaneously to the watcher's brain, shutting it down temporarily. Dwarfs were particularly susceptible to this kind of weapon, as they had a low light tolerance in the first place.

Artemis noticed the silver orb in Holly's hand.

"Butler," he said into his mike. "We need to get out of here! Now. Northeast corner."

He grabbed Mulch's collar, leading him backward. Overhead the canvas was falling, its descent cushioned by trapped air.

"We go," screamed Derph. "We go now. Leave everything and dig."

"You're not going anywhere," gasped Holly, her breath rasping along a bruised windpipe. She twisted the timer, rolling the grenade into the midst of the Significants. It was the perfect weapon against dwarfs. Shiny. No dwarf can resist anything shiny. Even Mulch was watching the glittering sphere, and would have kept watching until the flash, had Butler not slit a five-foot gash in the canvas and yanked the pair through the gap.

"Plan B," he grunted. "Next time we pay more attention to the backup strategy."

"Recriminations later," said Artemis briskly. "If Holly is here, then backup won't be far away. There must have been some kind of tracker on the helmet, something he hadn't detected. Perhaps in one of the coatings. "Here's the new plan. With the arrival of the LEP, we must split up now. I will write you a check for your share of the tiara. One point eight million euros, a fair black-market price."

"A check? Are you joking?" objected Mulch. "How do I know I can trust you, Mud Boy?"

"Believe me," said Artemis. "I am not to be trusted, generally. But we made a deal, and I don't cheat my partners. You could, of course, wait here for the LEP to arrive and discover your miraculous recovery from the usually fatal affliction of death."

Mulch snatched the offered check. "If this doesn't clear, then I'm coming to Fowl Manor, and remember I know how to get in." He noticed Butler's angry glare. "Though obviously, I hope it doesn't come to that."

"It won't. Trust me."

Mulch unbuttoned his bum flap. "It'd better not." He winked at Butler. And he was gone, below the earth in a flurry of dust, before the bodyguard could respond. It was just as well, really.

Artemis closed his fist around the blue diamond on the tiara's crown. It was already loose in its setting. All he had to do now was leave. Simple. Let the LEP clean up their own mess. But even before he heard Holly's voice, Artemis knew that it couldn't be that easy. Nothing ever was.

"Don't move, Artemis!" said the fairy captain. "I won't hesitate to shoot you. In fact, I'm quite looking forward to it."

Holly activated the Polaroid filter on her visor just before the stun grenade detonated. It was difficult to concentrate enough to perform even that simple operation. The canvas was flapping, the dwarfs were popping their bum flaps, and from the corner of her eye she noticed Fowl disappearing through a slit in the tent.

He would not escape again. This time she would get a mind-wipe warrant and erase the fairy People from the Irish boy's memory permanently.

She closed her eyes, in case any strobe light leaked through her visor, and waited for the pop. The flash, when it came, lit up the tent like a lampshade. Several seams of weak stitching were burned out, and rays of white light shot skyward like wartime searchlights. When she opened her eyes, the dwarfs were unconscious on the tent floor. One was the unfortunate Sergei, who had managed to climb from his tunnel just in time to get knocked out. Holly searched her belt for a sleeper-seeker hypodermic. The hypodermic contained small tracker beads loaded with a charged sedative. When the beads were injected into a fairy's bloodstream, that fairy could be tracked anywhere in the world, and knocked out at will. It made retrieving rogue fairies a lot easier. Holly quickly fought her way through the folds of canvas, tagged all six dwarfs, then crawled to the flaps. Now Sergei and his band could be apprehended at any time. This left her free to pursue Artemis Fowl.

The tent was around her ears now, held up by pockets of trapped air. She had to get out, or it would completely collapse on her. Holly activated the mechanical wings on her back, creating her own little wind tunnel, and hovered through the flap, boots scraping the earth.

Fowl was leaving along with Butler.

"Don't move, Artemis!" she yelled. "I won't hesitate to shoot you. In fact, I'm quite looking forward to it."

This was fighting talk, brimming with bravado and confidence—two things that were in short supply. But at least she sounded ready for a fight.

Artemis turned slowly. "Captain Short. You don't look so well. Maybe you should get some medical attention."

Holly knew she looked terrible. She could feel her fairy magic healing the bruises on her ribs, and her vision was still jumpy from stun-grenade overspill.

"I'm fine, Fowl. And even if I'm not, the computer in my helmet can fire this gun all on its own."

Butler took a step to one side, splitting the target.

He knew Holly would have to shoot him first.

"Don't bother, Butler," said Holly. "I can drop you and hunt the Mud Boy down in my own time."

Artemis tutted. "Time is something you don't have. The circus hands are already coming. In seconds they will be here, followed closely by the circus audience. Five hundred people all wondering what is going on here."

"So what? I'll be shielded."

"So there is no way for you to take me in. And even if you could, I doubt that I have broken any fairy law. All I did was to steal a human tiara. Surely the LEP don't get involved in human crime. I can't be held responsible for fairy criminals."

Holly struggled to keep her gun hand steady. Artemis was right, he hadn't done anything to threaten the People. And the shouts from the circus folk were growing louder.

"So you see, Holly, you have no choice but to let me go."

"And what about the other dwarf?"

"What dwarf?" said Artemis innocently.

"The seventh dwarf. There were seven."

Artemis counted on his fingers. "Six, I believe. Only six. Perhaps in all the excitement . . ."

Holly scowled behind her mask. There must be something she could salvage from this.

"Give me that tiara. And the helmet."

Artemis rolled the helmet across the ground. "The helmet, certainly. But the tiara is mine."

"Give it to me," shouted Holly, authority in every syllable. "Give it to me, or I will stun you both and you can take your chances with Ehrich Stern."

Artemis almost smiled. "Congratulations, Holly. A masterstroke." He took the tiara from his pocket, tossing it to the LEP officer.

"Now you can report that you broke up a gang of dwarf jewel thieves, and recovered the stolen tiara. A clutch of feathers in your cap, I would think."

People were coming. Their thumping feet jarred the earth.

Holly set her wings to hover.

"We'll meet again, Artemis Fowl," she said, rising into the air.

"I know," replied Artemis. "I look forward to it."

It was true. He did.

Artemis watched his nemesis lift slowly into the night sky. And just as the crowd appeared around the corner, she vibrated out of the visible spectrum. Only a fairy-shaped patch of stars remained.

Holly really makes things interesting, he thought, closing his fist around the stone in his pocket. I wonder if she will notice the switch. Will she look closely at the blue diamond and see that it seems a little bit oily?

Butler tapped him on the shoulder.

"Time to be gone," said the giant manservant.

Artemis nodded. Butler was right, as usual. He almost felt sorry for Sergei and the Significants. They would believe themselves safe right up until the Retrieval squad arrived to take them away.

Butler took his charge by the shoulder, and directed him to the shadows. In two steps they were invisible. Finding the darkness was a talent of Butler's.

Artemis looked skyward one last time. Where is Captain Short now? he wondered. In his mind she would always be there, looking over his shoulder, waiting for him to slip up.

EPİLOGUE

Fowl Manor

ANGELINE Fowl sat slumped at her dressing table, tears gathering at the corners of her eyes. Today was her husband's birthday. Little Arty's father, missing for over a year. Every day made his return more unlikely. Each day was difficult, but this day was almost impossible. She ran a slender finger over a photograph on the dresser. Artemis senior, with his strong teeth and blue eyes. Such a startling blue, she had never seen quite that color before or since, except in the eyes of her son. It had been the first thing she had noticed about him.

Artemis entered the room hesitantly. One foot outside the threshold.

"Arty, dear," said Angeline, drying her eyes. "Come here. Give me a hug, I need one."

Artemis crossed the deep pile carpet, remembering the many times he had seen his father framed by the bay window.

"I will find him," he whispered once he was in his mother's arms.

"I know you will, Arty," replied Angeline, fearful of the lengths her extraordinary son would go to. Afraid to lose another Artemis.

Artemis drew back. "I have a gift for you, Mother. Something to remind you, and give you strength."

He drew a golden chain from his breast pocket. Swinging in its V was the most incredible blue diamond. Angeline's breath caught in her throat. "Arty, it's uncanny. Amazing. That stone is exactly the same color . . ."

"As Father's eyes," completed Artemis, coupling

the clasp around his mother's neck. "I thought you might like it."

Angeline gripped the stone tightly in her hand, the tears flowing freely now. "I shall never take it off."

Artemis smiled sadly. "Trust me, Mother, I will find him."

Angeline looked at her son in wonder. "I know you will, Arty," she said again. But this time, she believed it.

Don't miss the thrilling
new futuristic adventure

by EOIN COLFER

THE SUPERNATURALIST

AT THE CLARISSA FRAYNE INSTITUTE for Parentally Challenged Boys, every day was basically the same. Toil by day, fitful sleep by night. There were no days off, no juvenile rights. Every day was a workday. The marshals worked the orphans so hard that by eight P.M. most of the boys were asleep standing up, dreaming of their beds.

Cosmo Hill was the exception. He spent every moment of his waking life watching for that one chance. That split second when his freedom would beckon to him from outside an unlocked door, or an unguarded fence. He must be ready to seize that moment and run with it.

It wasn't likely that his chance would come on this particular day. And even if it did, Cosmo didn't think he would have the energy to run anywhere.

The no-sponsors had spent the afternoon testing a new series of antiperspirants. Their legs had been shaved and sectioned with rings of tape. The flesh between the bands was sprayed with five varieties of antiperspirant, and then the boys were set on treadmills and told to run. Sensors attached to their legs monitored their sweat glands, determining which spray was most effective. By the end of the day, Cosmo had run six miles, and the pores on his legs were inflamed and scalding. He was almost glad to be cuffed to a moving partner and begin the long walk back to the dormitory.

Each boy had a section in the dorm where he ate, slept, and passed whatever leisure time the no-sponsors had. These rooms were actually sections of cardboard utility pipe that had been sawed into six-foot lengths. The pipes were suspended on a network of wires almost fifty feet off the ground. Once the pipes were occupied by orphans, the entire contraption swayed like an ocean liner.

Cosmo climbed quickly, ignoring the pain in his leg muscles. His pipe was near the top. If the lights went out before he reached it, he could be stranded on the ladder.

After a few minutes of feverish climbing, Cosmo reached his level. A narrow walkway, barely the width of his hand, serviced each pipe. Cosmo slid across carefully, gripping a rail on the underside of the walkway above him. His pipe was four columns across. Cosmo swung inside, landing on the foam rubber mattress. Ten seconds later, the lights went out.

Someone knocked gently on the pipe above. It was Ziplock Murphy. The network was opening up. Cosmo answered the knock with one of his own, then pulled back his mattress, signaling Fence in the pipe below. The no-sponsors had developed a system of communication that allowed them to converse without angering the marshals. Clarissa Frayne discouraged actual face-to-face communication between the boys, on the grounds that friendships might develop. And friendships could lead to unity, maybe even revolt.

Cosmo dug his nails into a seam in the cardboard pipe and pulled out two small tubes. Both had been fashioned from mashed gum bottle and crispbread, then baked on a windowsill. Cosmo screwed one into a small hole in the base of his pipe, and the other into a hole overhead.

Ziplock's voice wafted through from above. "Hey, Cosmo. How are your legs?"

"Burning," grunted Cosmo. "I put my gum bottle on one, but it's not helping."

"I tried that too," said Fence from below. "Antiperspirants. This is nearly as bad as the time they had us testing those Creeper slugs. I was throwing up for a week."

Comments and suggestions snuck through the holes from all over the pipe construct. The fact that the pipes were all touching, along with the acoustics of the hall, meant that voices traveled amazing distances through the network. Cosmo could hear no-sponsors whispering almost three hundred fifty feet away.

"What does the Chemist say?" asked Cosmo. "About our legs?"

The Chemist was the orphanage name for a boy three columns across. He loved to watch medical programs on TV and was the closest the no-sponsors had to a consultant.

Word came back in under a minute. "The Chemist says spit on your hands and rub it in. The spit has some kind of salve in it. Don't lick your fingers, though, or the antiperspirant will make you sicker than those Creeper slugs."

The sound of boys spitting echoed through the hall. The entire lattice of pipes shook with their efforts. Cosmo followed the Chemist's advice, then lay back, letting a hundred different conversations wash over him. Sometimes he would join in, or at least listen to one of Ziplock's yarns. But tonight all he could think about was that moment when freedom would beckon to him. And being ready when it arrived.

Also from Eoin Colfer
comes an exciting tale of life, death
and the unexpected hereafter